DESTINY OF THE LIZARDSTONE SCEPTER

A DRAGONSTONE STORY, BOOK IV

BY
MARK M. EVEN

Inspired by, and additional material by,
Gina L. Even

CRESTINGWAVE
PUBLISHING

DESTINY OF THE LIZARDSTONE SCEPTER
A Dragonstone Story, Book IV

Written by Mark M. Even
Inspired by, and additional material by, Gina Even

Published by Cresting Wave Publishing, LLC, 2025.

"We print the books you need to read."

ISBN: 978-1-956048-98-8

Edited by Kris Neely
Book Design & Layout by Lazar Kackarovski

TABLE OF CONTENTS

**Dedicated to all the
Even children and grandchildren.**

Thank you to our reviewers!

DESCENDANTS OF PHEF
– FAMILY TREE

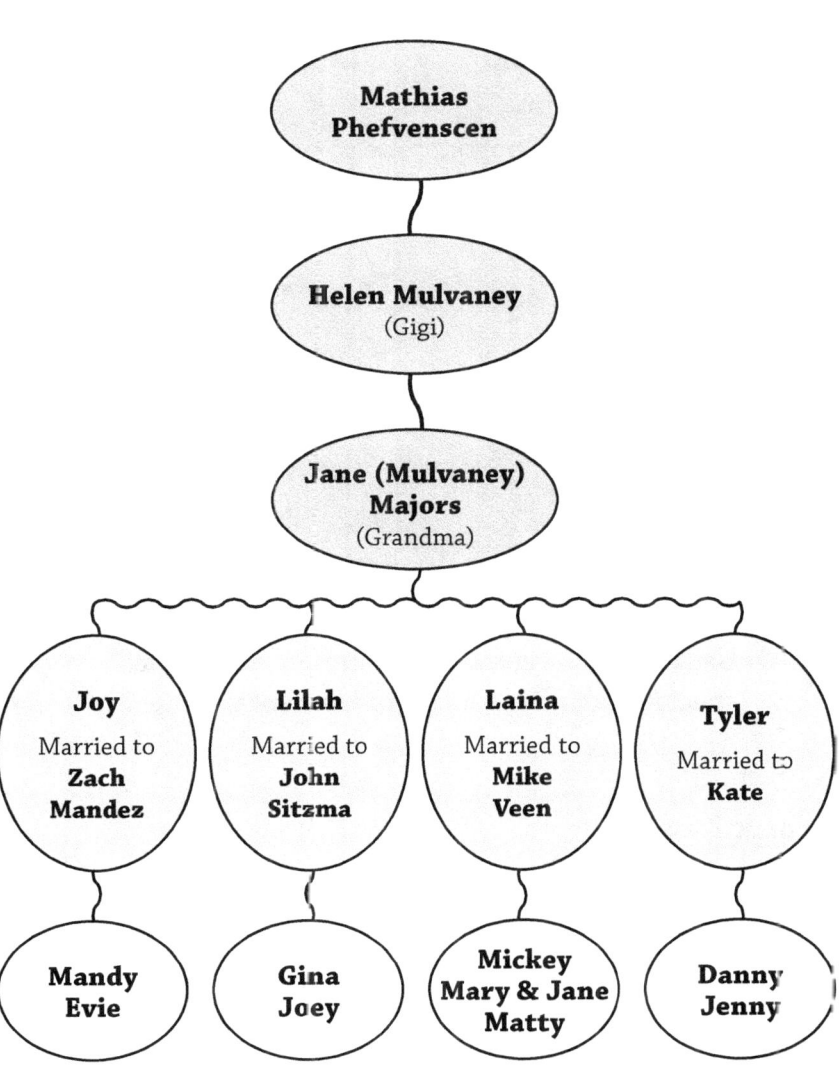

CAST OF CHARACTERS

Danny Majors

- Codename: 'Onyx'
- Mandy's cousin
- Uses his black Dragonstone to power his magic, capable of changing the composition of objects
- Age: 12

Delores Sparks

- Mother to Gail Sparks
- Neighbor and friend to Grandma

Evie Mandez

- Codename: 'Aqua'
- Mandy's younger sister
- Uses a blue Dragonstone to power her magic, specializes in the control of elements
- Age: 10

Frank Lange

- Wizard and professional thief
- Deceased
- Previous owner of Mandy's Lizardstone ring

Gail Sparks

- FBI Agent and team leader of the FDM

Gigi (Helen Mulvaney)

- Mother of Grandma
- No magical powers
- Deceased and existing in Owya

Gina Sitzma

- Codename: 'Spyglass'
- Mandy's cousin
- Uses a red Dragonstone to power her magic, specializes in extraordinary senses, including a healing touch
- Age: 13

Grandma (Jane Majors)

- Mother of Joy, Lilah, Laina, & Tyler
- No magical powers
- Family matriarch

Green Hand (Kijani M'kono)

- Witch doctor and wizard

Hugh Blackman

- FBI Agent

J.T. ("Justin Valeigh")

- Magician from Storyworld who returned to Earth and joined the family as their magical teacher and mentor

Jane Veen

- Codename: 'J-Cat / Gemini'
- Uses her yellow Dragonstone to merge with her twin sister (Mary) and transform into Gemini- a giant, winged/icefire-breathing two-headed tiger
- Age: 8

Jenny Majors

- Codename: 'Prism'
- Danny's little sister
- Uses a diamond Dragonstone to transform into a living diamond humanoid capable of invisibility and use of light
- Also invulnerable and indestructible, with no need of air or food when in diamond form
- Age: 9

Joey Sitzma

- Codename: 'Atlas'
- Gina's brother
- Powered by a pearl Dragonstone fueled by moonlight, turns into a super-strong giant
- Age: 9

John Sitzma

- Maintains facilities of the M-Force and FDM
- Gina's father
- Non-magical
- Construction and carpentry by trade

Joy Mandez

- Codename: 'Cash'
- Mandy's mother
- Uses a yellow Dragonstone to power her magic
- Accountant by trade

Khammy Pakiko, Commander

- Naval captain of the FDM ship Warbird

Kate Majors

- Codename: 'Doc'
- Danny's mother
- Non-magical
- Medical doctor by trade

Laina Veen

- Codename: 'Jewel'
- Mickey's mother, Joy's younger sister, Lilah's twin sister
- Uses a pink Dragonstone to power her magic
- Jeweler by trade

Lilah Sitzma

- Codename: 'Teach'
- Gina's mother, Joy's younger sister, Laina's twin sister
- Uses a pink Dragonstone to power her magic
- A teacher by trade

Loganna

- Sorceress
- Deceased and existing in Owya

Lu Long

- Sorceress and gun runner/smuggler
- Deceased
- Previous owner of Mandy's Lizardstone amulet

Mandy Mandez

- Codename: 'Oz'
- De facto leader, most powerful witch of the M-Force team
- Uses a blue Dragonstone and two green Lizardstones to power her magic
- Daughter of Joy and Zach Mandez
- Age: 13

Mary Veen

- Codename: 'M-Cat / Gemini'
- Uses her red Dragonstone to merge with her twin sister (Jane) and transform into Gemini - a giant, winged/ice/fire-breathing two-headed tiger
- Age: 8

Matty Veen

- Codename: 'Casper'
- Uses his clear crystal Dragonstone to enter Owya (the Spirit World)
- Age: 6

Mickey Veen

- Codename: 'Bamf'
- Mandy's cousin
- Uses a purple Dragonstone to power his magic, capable of teleportation
- Age: 13

Mike Veen

- Codename: 'Judge'
- Mickey's father
- Non-magical
- Lawyer by trade
- Heads administration of the M-Force

Phef the Wizard (Mathias Phefenscen)

- Ancient ancestor of Grandma and her blood descendants
- Wizard of extraordinary powers
- Deceased and existing in Owya, the spirit world

Thena

- A Golden dragon
- Leader of all dragons

Tyler Majors

- Codename: 'Shaq'
- Danny's father, younger brother of Joy, Laina, & Lilah
- Uses a silver Dragonstone to power his magic
- Software engineer by trade

Vanessa Chen

- FBI Agent

Wylee Conners

- FBI Agent

Zach Mandez

- Codename: 'Engineer'
- Mandy's father
- Non-magical
- Electrical engineer and computer scientist by trade

Zilla

- A Giant Lizard
- Leader of the lizard herd that is under Mandy's Queendom

PROLOGUE

A LONG TIME AGO, A young orphan boy lived on the streets of a small village. His name was Mathias Phefvenscen, but the villagers called him Matty. He survived on handouts, slept against the village wall, and sometimes stole food to stay alive.

While searching for berries in the woods one evening, Matty heard a commotion ahead. Creeping through the trees, he found a group of men in a circle. They were punching and kicking something trapped in their midst. Though the cries didn't sound human, they tore at Matty's heart.

"Leave it alone!" Matty shouted, bursting through the trees with a large stick in hand.

Before anyone could react, he struck one man on the shoulder, knocking him into another and creating a gap. A yellow-colored animal dashed through the opening so quickly Matty couldn't see what it was in the dim light. The men's faces turned angry. Matty ran in the same direction as the animal, with the men close behind. Being younger and quicker, he outpaced them, turning left and scrambling up a tree. As the men rushed below, Matty's dirty clothes helped hide him against the trunk.

"I recognized that boy! It was that street-rat called Matty!" one man shouted. As their voices faded, Matty relaxed.

"Thank you be saving me, young one," said a soft, gravelly voice from above.

Matty nearly fell from his hiding place. Looking up, he could barely see a light-colored shape in the darkness.

"Wha... who are you?" Matty asked nervously.

"You can call me Paction," came the reply. "What name do you go by?" Afraid to give his real name, Matty paused before answering, "You can call me Phef."

The creature shifted position and snorted. "They be coming back—with more men and torches! Quickly, climb down and run be far from the village as possible. Then run even farther after you rest! It is not safe for you around here."

As Matty began climbing down, he heard shouting getting closer. He looked up and whispered, "What about you?"

"I be lead them away in the other direction," the creature replied. "Now, be go!"

Matty ran from the mob's voices. He stopped to catch his breath on a trail leading to another village. Then, he spotted torch flames to his left. He dropped to the ground to avoid being seen. Eventually, the flames disappeared into the distance, and he ran as far as he could through the darkness.

ii.

Several years passed. Matty roamed the countryside, taking on odd jobs to earn a living. Afraid of being recognized, he continued using the name 'Phef.' He stopped stealing, fearing capture. He grew to be over six feet tall and developed a full beard. Eventually, feeling safer from being identified as "street-rat Matty," he settled in the village of Talon.

The baron who lived outside Talon hired Matty as a shepherd. Along with two other men, Matty watched over the sheep at night, guarding against wolves and thieves. He carried a sturdy staff carved from oak, soaked in tree sap, then dried and polished until it was hard and shiny. While the other shepherds dozed one night, Matty spotted a brief flame on a nearby hill. He woke the others and ran toward the fire. He smelled burnt wool and meat. As he reached the hilltop, he dropped to his knees and crawled over the crest.

The other shepherds sprinted past him, yelling and waving their staffs. Flames shot over their heads, and they bolted back toward camp, shrieking in terror. Matty watched them flee and started to join them when he felt scorching air above his head—like sticking his head in a furnace.

He slowly turned to face the threat, ready to strike with his staff. He stumbled back in terror. An immense golden dragon stood over him. It opened its jaws as if to eat him but then shook its majestic head. Moving its face toward Matty, it took a deep sniff.

"Phef?" it said in a deep, gravelly voice. "Is that be you?"

"Ye... yes," Matty replied weakly. "I am Phef."

"It's be me," the dragon said with surprising softness, "... Paction!"

"But... you're a dragon!" Matty said, slowly standing up.

"Of course, I'm be dragon, you dolt!" replied Paction. "What else be?"

The dragon sat on the grass beside Matty, its head still towering over him. Matty also sat down, and they talked about that fateful night years ago when Matty had saved the young creature. Finally, Paction stood and said, "You be courageous that night, Phef. Attacking those be men to save a dragon you didn't be know. It be so: owe you my life, I do young Phef, and I be a gift for you."

"A gift?" Matty asked. "What can a dragon give a man?"

"I sense great magic be within you," Paction replied. "You have the makings of a powerful wizard, but you be no way to tap the magic. I be help." After a pause, Paction continued, "Phef, be you any gold or silver?"

Matty shook his head no, then remembered and pulled a small gold coin from his pocket. "It's all I have. I've been saving it to buy a gift for the baron's daughter, hoping she might like me." Matty smiled slightly. "Her name is Loganna."

Paction said, "Put be coin on the ground. Be back away." Reluctantly, Matty obeyed.

He watched as Paction lowered its head almost to the coin. A golden flame shot from the dragon's mouth, growing brighter and brighter until it stopped. Matty stepped forward and reached for the coin.

"Wait!" Paction said softly. "Wait, be it cool."

Matty watched as steam faded around his coin. In place of the small gold coin sat a brilliant white jewel.

"That be Dragonstone," said Paction. "Its magical properties be let you tap inner magic and perform spells and charms be."

"I don't know any spells or charms!" exclaimed Matty. "What good will this be?"

"Ah, you be know them! Just be touch the Dragonstone," Paction explained.

Matty picked up the stone with his right hand. Immediately, it glowed with a brilliant white light that grew so intense it turned Matty's hair, beard, and even his clothes, pure white.

And at that moment, Matty became Phef the Wizard!

iii.

For the next eight years, Phef used his magic to help the villagers and royals in the kingdom of Cladiclad. His magical skills grew stronger with experience. Once, in a northern corner of Cladiclad, Phef visited the small village of Brony.

He stopped at an old inn called the Brony Bear—the only place for miles where travelers could find a warm bed or meal. An old couple named Erik and Georgina Barson ran the inn.

The Barsons had no children, but years ago, they'd taken in a young orphan boy found asleep on their doorstep. While mostly kind to him, they worked him hard. The boy couldn't recall his name, so they called him 'Boy.' He grew quickly and helped around the inn with various chores—cleaning the dining area and helping in the kitchen—but the miserly Barsons never paid him anything, just room and board. Over time, Boy longed to leave. So, he planned to save enough money to set out on his own. He began stealing from drunk patrons and became quite good at pickpocketing.

That night, Phef watched as Boy delivered a bowl of onion soup. Boy noticed a drunk man had fallen asleep at a table across the room, with his money bag sticking out of his coat. Boy saw his chance for a big score. And escape!

As Phef observed, Boy casually walked among the tables, collecting dirty dishes as he approached the unsuspecting patron. When he reached the drunk, he bumped against him slightly, grabbed the money bag, and tucked it into his shirt. The drunk opened one eye, and Boy apologized profusely. But as he did, Boy's leg knocked against a chair behind him, and he fell hard onto the stone floor. Dishes, glasses, and silver coins scattered everywhere.

Fully awakened by the noise, the drunk spotted his money bag and immediately accused Boy of stealing. Then the drunk noticed other patrons rushing to pick up coins from the floor! In the chaos, Boy burst out the back door, running for his life, with the innkeeper shouting for him never to return. About a mile away, Boy finally stopped, out of breath and bleeding from a cut above his eye. He bent over with hands on his knees, trying to catch his breath.

"That was a close one, young man," said a voice behind him. "If they had caught you, they might have hung you for your thievery." Startled, Boy turned quickly and threw a punch, but it hit nothing. There was no one there! The voice came from behind him again: "What is your name?"

Boy turned back more cautiously and saw the bearded man from the inn. "I have no name. Everyone just calls me 'Boy,'" he replied.

"My name is Mathias Phefvenscen," the old man said. "I'm looking for someone to be my valet, and if he proves worthy, perhaps he can become my apprentice."

"What's a valet?" Boy asked.

"Pick up my bags and follow me, and you'll find out," Phef replied with a smile.

Boy looked down and saw two travel bags on the ground. *I'm sure those weren't there before*, he thought. He looked up to see the old man already walking down the road. Boy shrugged, picked up the bags, and followed. Just as he started thinking about how to steal from the old man, Phef said, "Put those ideas out of your mind, Boy!"

Amazed, Boy decided he'd better stick with the old guy and take his chances.

iv.

Over the years, Boy learned that Mathias Phefvenscen was the famous Phef the Wizard and devoted himself to being his valet and aide. Once, Phef gave him a small white Dragonstone, hoping to teach him to use inner magic, but Boy couldn't tap any magic through the stone. However, Boy was very skilled at learning spells and charms. He could tap the natural magic surrounding all living beings, the Earth, and the Heavens. Phef tutored the boy into becoming a powerful young wizard and kept him as his apprentice for several years.

As Phef and his valet roamed the Cladiclad kingdom, he especially cared for his village of Talon while also courting

Loganna, the beautiful daughter of Talon's baron. After their courtship, Phef married Loganna, and eventually, they had a child named Mandalina.

Over the years, one of Phef's greatest accomplishments was allying with the dragons. Phef and the golden dragon queen, Paction, had been friends since Phef had saved her life years before. Because of this alliance, the dragons agreed to stop eating sheep, pigs, and cattle owned by villagers and promised to eat only wild game, such as elk, deer, or boars.

But as dragons began hunting in the forests, they occasionally caused problems with the other occupants: giant lizards! To flush animals from dense foliage, dragons used their fiery breath. Unfortunately, they often accidentally burned the Red Azara bushes. Giant lizards ate only fruit from the Red Azara bushes, and each bush was precious to them.

So, the lizards began defending the bushes by fighting any dragon that came near, sometimes, unfortunately, killing young dragons with their blazing green fireballs.

Phef arranged a meeting between Paction and the lizard queen, Drof, to prevent war between dragons and giant lizards. He chose a neutral spot in a field near his cottage in the rolling hills of Cladiclad. As Phef waited outside, his wife Loganna stayed inside, holding their young daughter.

Phef heard Loganna cooing, "My sweet little Mandy. How I love you so." Phef smiled at the pet name "Mandy" and felt love for his daughter and wife rise within him. He had just turned to go inside to kiss his daughter when he heard Paction's wings as she landed in the nearby field. Instead, he smiled at his family and greeted the dragon.

"Hello, dear friend," he called out. "Are you prepared to make peace with the lizards?"

"Hello, Phef," replied Paction. "I be prepared, but be Drof?"

"We shall soon see," said Phef, pointing toward the woods beyond the field.

A giant green lizard, nearly as large as the dragon, emerged from the woods. Its tongue flicked in and out as it approached. Phef asked Paction to stay put while he approached the lizard, who stopped and waited. Phef heard a raspy voice in his mind: "Well, wizard, be the dragons ready to stay out of our forest?"

Paction roared, hearing the same voice, "It be not your forest, demon! The forest belongs to no one. Therefore, it belongs to all!

Phef raised his hands and palms toward each creature, trying to signal them to stop. "Please, my friends. We're here to discuss your differences, not trade accusations." Then, to the lizard, he said, "Drof, the dragons will avoid using flames near Red Azara bushes if they can see them. But that means you can no longer hide the bushes."

Drof's reply echoed in their minds: "If we don't conceal them, unicorns will find and eat the fruit. We must protect our food at any cost. This is a waste of time! I knew I couldn't trust a dragon to be reasonable!"

Before Phef could react, the dragon leaped over him, reaching out to stop the lizard from leaving. The lizard turned at that moment, and the dragon's claw tore into its shoulder. Drof cried in pain and spun around, shooting a flaming fireball at the dragon. Paction raised her golden wing to block it, but the fireball bounced to the right—directly toward Phef's cottage! Phef turned in horror as the fireball struck the corner of the cottage just as Loganna stepped through the front door.

"NO!" Phef cried as his wife's screams filled the air. As he ran toward the cottage, the lizard retreated into the woods, leaving

Paction alone in the field. When Phef reached his wife, who knelt sobbing on the ground, he saw the devastation: the entire west corner of the cottage—where his daughter's bedroom was—had been destroyed and was burning.

"I had just laid her down when I heard the commotion," Loganna cried between sobs. "I was worried about you! But look what happened!"

She stood, and Phef saw rage in her eyes. "This is YOUR FAULT! You always think you have to do good! This time, you did nothing good! This time, you tore my heart from my body and stomped on it!" Then she ran toward the woods.

Unable to move, Phef called after her, "Wait, Loganna! Where are you going?" As she entered the woods, he heard her answer, "To kill the beast that killed the flesh of my flesh!"

By then, Paction had approached Phef. She lowered her head and hissed, "I am terribly sorry. I be go now. I think it best if my dragon clan be find another kingdom to live in, away from the lizards and from you and your wife."

Phef nodded silently as tears ran down his face. Hours later, he finally turned away from his burned-down cottage. He could have stopped the fire, but he knew he had nothing left there. He retreated to a cave in the hills, sat in the middle, and closed his eyes as he chanted a spell. When he finished, he froze solid, his eyes merging into a single, glowing white orb. Phef couldn't move or be moved. In this state, he needed no food or drink.

He could see only Loganna and everything she did in his magical mind's eye.

v.

Loganna tracked the lizard that had fired the deadly fireball for over two years. She mastered archery and killed many giant lizards, finding none with the shoulder scar from the dragon's claw. She also learned to throw a bola—a weapon of rope and stone that, when thrown correctly, would tangle around the legs of any creature to trap it. Phef watched as Loganna raged through the kingdom, killing every giant lizard she found.

Finally, he saw her throw a bola around Drof's legs, causing her to fall to the ground. She wrapped another bola around Drof's mouth, preventing her from shooting fireballs. Then he watched her torture Drof with precisely aimed arrows that caused pain but didn't kill. Finally, Drof begged mercy with her mind-voice: "Loganna, please, be no more. If you spare me, I be give you my heart, which will give you magical powers that rival Phef's. Just be stop! Please!"

"Your heart?" Phef heard Loganna say. "Yes, I will take your heart just as you took mine. Give it to me, and I will end your pain."

Phef watched as Drof struggled to move a paw to her chest, then extended a single claw and cut a slit. The giant lizard's throbbing green heart spilled out. "There," Drof's voice echoed. "If you hold the heart in your hand, it be give you power and I continue to... NOOOO!"

Loganna picked up a large rock and smashed it down on the green heart, shattering it into five pieces of stone. With her heart destroyed, Drof burst into flames and turned to dust. Loganna picked up the largest fragment, and a green aura glowed around her, temporarily blinding Phef's magic eye.

When the aura cleared, Phef saw a transformed Loganna with flowing green hair, standing tall and roaring like a giant lizard. The entire lizard herd emerged from the forest and surrounded her in minutes. Loganna scooped up the other four Lizardstones, held them above her head, and declared, "I have slain your queen! Bow to me now, for I am Loganna, the Lizard Queen!"

Phef awoke from his spell at that moment and said, "Oh, no. Loganna, what have you become?"

vi.

By defeating the lizard queen, Loganna now ruled the entire herd. By bonding with the Lizardstones, she became a powerful witch. Over time, as the Lizardstones connected with her inner magic and emotions, Loganna went mad with rage and grief from her daughter's death. Eventually, she set out to rule the kingdom of Cladiclad, knowing that to do so, she must defeat her former husband.

She blamed Phef for her daughter's death and grew even more enraged when she learned Phef had remarried a young woman from Talon and started a new family. Loganna went on a rampage, attacking villages throughout the land and practicing her magic to become powerful enough to defeat Phef. Using her magic to spy on him, she attacked the village of Talon when she saw he had taken his family away.

Without Phef to protect the village, she easily defeated the castle guards and killed all who opposed her. Even though the village baron was her father, she ransacked the castle and took whatever she wanted. She found her father hiding in his throne room and demanded he tell her where Phef had gone. When her father tried to hit her with his golden scepter, she struck him down with a blast of green energy from her Lizardstone. Loganna picked up the scepter as she watched her father take his last breath. Since the scepter was rightfully hers, she used it to hold all five Lizardstones.

Loganna went to the burning stables and found the blacksmith among the wreckage. She told him she would spare his life if he forged a new top for the scepter to hold the Lizardstones—the largest in the middle, with the other four surrounding it. She ordered her lizards to watch him and gave him one night to complete the task.

Loganna returned to the castle and ordered the terrified villagers to prepare a feast and celebration in her honor. Too scared to refuse, the villagers obeyed while Loganna's giant lizards watched. Loganna and the villagers ate and drank themselves into a stupor at the feast.

vii.

Months later, as Loganna raided another village, Phef the Wizard appeared suddenly to stop her. Loganna fought Phef, using the power of her scepter with its five Lizardstones, and forced him to retreat. But, as she prepared to launch one last attack, a familiar feeling in her stomach made her pause, allowing Phef to escape. *A baby?* She thought. *How could that be?* Then she remembered the drunken party at Talon castle. Her spirits lifted at the thought of having another child—perhaps filling the terrible hole in her soul since her daughter's death.

Loganna hid in the forest, protected by the giant lizard herd, until her baby was born. After a long, painful labor, her child arrived—and Loganna was outraged that it was a boy! She had wanted a girl to replace what she had lost. Angered and disappointed, she abandoned the baby in the forest and set out to conquer the rest of Cladiclad.

Shortly after she and her lizards left, Phef appeared in the forest. He had been watching her with his magic eye, hoping to find a way to defeat her and end her terror. Phef rescued the baby boy and took him to the village of Brony, where a young childless couple had recently taken over the local inn. Phef left the baby with them to raise as their own, warning that he would keep a close eye to ensure they were good parents. He didn't tell them whose child it was, and the couple promised to love and raise the boy as best they could.

Afterward, Phef traveled to a hidden valley, concealed by his magic, where his family and valet lived. Phef summoned his dragon friend, Paction, and together, they planned to end Loganna's reign of terror once and for all.

As planned, when Loganna appeared at another village, Phef transported there to confront her. "Loganna," he called, "You must stop this senseless destruction! It is me you want revenge against! Come, let's battle together and put an end to this!"

Loganna's response was a green firebolt that Phef easily blocked. She commanded her lizards to attack, but they all stopped as an entire army of dragons magically appeared.

Phef shouted to the lizards, "The dragons will not fight you if you will not fight them. Loganna is not one of you! You owe her no loyalty!"

When Loganna saw the lizards back off and stand still, she became outraged. She rushed at Phef, holding her scepter like a lance and shooting firebolts from its tip.

Phef stood perfectly still, protected by an unseen force, and raised his staff above his head with both hands. As Loganna neared him, a burst of energy from behind struck her directly in the back, stopping her firebolts in midair. Stunned, she stumbled closer to Phef just as he smashed his staff down, striking the scepter at its top. A massive burst of energy exploded from the scepter, knocking everyone to the ground.

From behind Loganna, Phef's apprentice emerged and said, "Your plan worked, Master."

"Not quite, my lad," Phef responded. "It seems the scepter still holds the main Lizardstone. What became of the other four stones, I couldn't guess. Perhaps they'll turn up someday. But now, we must deal with Loganna."

"Someone should destroy her for all the death and destruction she has caused," the apprentice said.

"That, I cannot do," Phef answered solemnly. "For now, I think it best to banish her to a place she can never escape." Phef began to chant a spell that would transport Loganna to a different dimension and place her in an endless trance until he could bring her back and free her spirit from the anger. Just as he finished the spell, Loganna regained consciousness and summoned her scepter to her hand, but it was too late to use it. She disappeared from the world.

Phef spent the rest of his years repairing the damage Loganna had caused, helping people throughout the land rebuild their lives. As he grew older, he also enjoyed his family, watching them grow and become good stewards of the land and their magic.

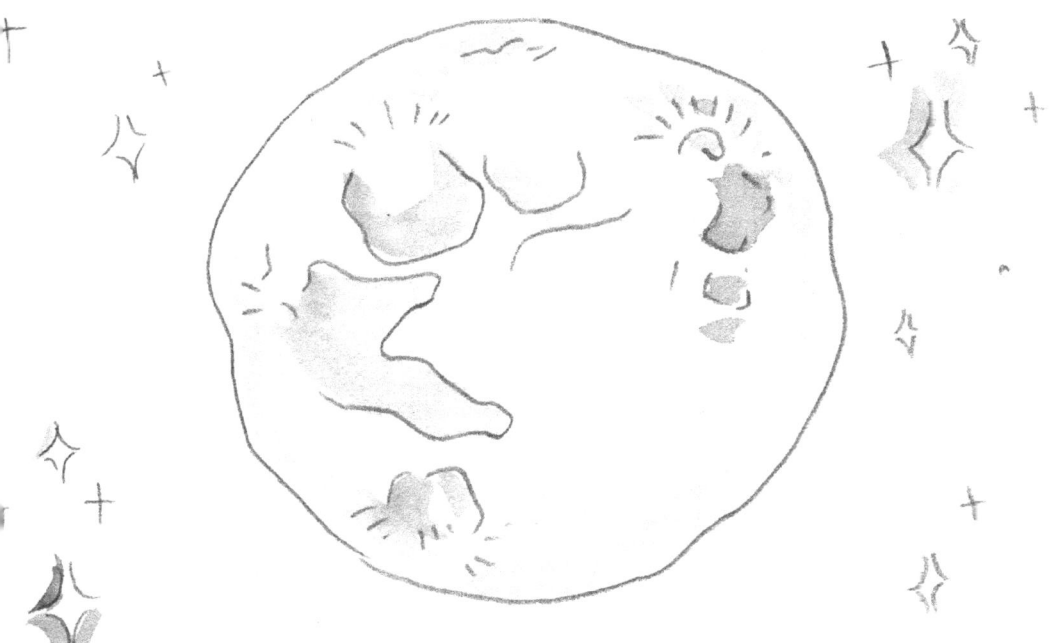

CHAPTER 1

LUNAR 1

ANDY'S BOOTS CRUNCHED INTO the gray lunar dust as she tightened the last bolt on the Oxy-ginator. She watched the device's status light pulse from amber to steady green through her helmet's visor. Success! The machine hummed to life, already beginning to create breathable oxygen for *LUNAR 1*, humanity's first permanent Moon base.

"Status check, Oz," her father's voice crackled through her helmet comm. Even after six months of space missions, hearing him use her astronaut call sign still made her smile.

"Final installation complete," Mandy replied, carefully standing up in the bulky silver spacesuit. "Ready for transport home, Engineer."

The vast lunar landscape stretched before her—craters and mountains under a pitch-black sky. *"Well,"* she thought, *"this sure beats doing homework!"* That was life for a thirteen-year-old who happened to be both an astronaut and a magician. Anyway, it was time to go home.

A familiar tingling sensation washed over her as the transportation spell activated. Through her helmet, she glimpsed the shimmering blue portal materializing beside them. The Complex Command Center's (CCC) voice cut through their comms: "Transporting now!"

"Roger that," Agent Wylee Conners replied. The tall, muscular, brown-haired man quickly stood up from his cluttered operations desk and walked to the far end of the CCC, just as a shimmering, light blue portal opened next to a dark blue post in the center of the Teleportation Area. Two silver-suited astronauts materialized and walked through the portal. The gold-bordered name tag on the larger of the two astronauts read "Engineer"; on the smaller astronaut behind him, it read "Oz." The Engineer turned around and reached for the bulky helmet on Oz. "Here, Mandy, let me help you with that." The release mechanisms hissed as he twisted it free.

Shaking her head free of the helmet's black compression collar, Mandy replied, "Gracias, Papi."

In the weightlessness of space, astronaut suits and oxygen tanks have a trivial effect on movement. But on Earth, they are, to say the least, heavy and bulky, and Mandy always wanted to be unburdened from the weight as soon as possible. Before she could offer to help her dad, Agent Conners assisted with removing the Engineer's helmet. Then he helped them remove their heavy space suits. The light blue poly flight suits they wore under their space suits were much more comfortable!

Agent Conners glanced up from unfastening Mandy's boots, a faint smirk tugging at his lips. "So, what's the Moon like? Bet Earth feels heavier already."

"Everything went perfectly," Mandy's dad replied. Mandy's 'Oxy-ginators' and 'Aqua-ginators' are now operational. Next, NASA must run a month's worth of tests before populating *LUNAR 1*.

Mandy stretched, trying to work out the stiffness in her shoulders. The recycled air of the Complex carried the sharp tang of ozone from the portal, mixed with the metallic scent that always lingered after space missions. She was just reaching for her red sneakers when a familiar voice called from the doorway.

"You okay?" Gina appeared in the doorway, concern etched on her face. "Mom said you looked wiped out after shrinking that entire building."

"I'm fine," Mandy said, but her voice betrayed her exhaustion. "Just need to adjust. You know how it is - one minute you're bouncing around the Moon, the next you're trying to remember how walking normally works."

"Well, you'd better remember fast," Gina grinned. "Grandma's expecting us; you know how she gets when we're late. Plus, she's making her specialty — Irish stew."

"Space mission to Grandma's stew," Mandy laughed, then groaned as her muscles protested. "Sometimes I forget that most thirteen-year-olds don't have to balance homework with lunar construction projects."

"Most thirteen-year-olds can't turn wood into titanium either," her dad said, gently squeezing her shoulder. "Go on. Take a shower, get changed. Family time is just as important as saving the world."

Evie's voice echoed through the complex as if on cue: "Move it, Mandy! I'm hungry!"

"Welcome back to Earth," Gina teased. "Where the gravity is heavy, and the little sisters are impatient."

Agent Conners gave Mandy's dad a thumbs-up and wandered back to his station, his boots squeaking against the freshly polished floor. The familiar scent of coffee wafted from his desk—*probably his third cup of the day,* Mandy thought. She'd started noticing how all the adults here practically lived on caffeine.

Mandy slumped against the cool metal wall, her muscles still protesting Earth's gravity. She marveled at what they'd accomplished in the past six months. The past six months felt like something out of a movie — the kind she and Gina used to binge-watch on weekend sleepovers.

It all started when Mandy, her cousins Danny and Jenny, traveled to the Moon to rescue three stranded astronauts. On that trip, Mandy promised to take Danny and Jenny's mom to space after they returned. However, Mandy, the M-Force, and the FDM battled the evil sorceress Lu Long, thus delaying those plans. The memory sent a chill down her spine despite the Complex's carefully regulated temperature.

Luckily, they survived the intense battle. She absently traced the warm metal of Lu Long's Lizardstone amulet at her throat. With that victory, Mandy employed Frank Lange's Lizardstone ring and the amulet, which dramatically increased her magical power when used with Mandy's Dragonstone wand. The Lizardstone ring on her finger pulsed faintly as if responding to her thoughts.

Eventually, Mandy kept her promise and took Aunt Kate up to space. Mandy discovered, in doing so, that she could "sense" a beacon she had left inside the spaceship *Aquarius I's lunar lander*. Using her magic, she had "enchanted" the silver-and-black captain's chair inside the lunar lander, enabling easy transport back to it and saving stranded astronauts on the Moon. But she also quickly lost her magical connection to the chair when they blasted out of the Moon's orbit to return to Earth.

But now, with her increased magical power, she found she could sense the beacon from Earth's orbit! This meant she could transport herself to the Moon from there, which was great. Not so great was the fact that the Earth's ozone and some radiation layers prevented her from connecting to the beacon from the ground, so she first had to transport to space—and then transport again to the Moon.

A shout from her brown-haired younger sister, Evie, broke through her thoughts. "Mandy, hurry! Remember, we're going on a girls' trip back to Grandma's house for the weekend!"

"I'll catch up!" Mandy called back, watching them disappear in a flash that left purple spots dancing in her vision. She could almost smell Grandma's Irish stew already—way better than the freeze-dried space food she'd been eating all week.

Mandy recalled how she approached the Director of the FDM with her idea to work with NASA to create a lunar outpost. It took a little convincing, but with orders from the President on crisp ivory-colored letterhead, NASA made the *LUNAR 1* project. Mandy's plan consisted of creating a set of portals — one from NASA to a stationary space station just above the Earth and one from the space station to the Moon.

To prove it could be done, Mandy and Astronaut Tommy Streff (one of the astronauts she had rescued from the Moon, a short, barrel-chested Irishman with a close-cropped red beard to match his hair) were first transported to a satellite in Earth's orbit and then to the lunar lander. With that, Astronaut Streff reported to NASA that, indeed, the plan had worked perfectly.

Mandy had to grin, remembering NASA's reaction when they realized they needed a satellite big enough for actual people. All those PhDs were scratching their heads while she and Astronaut Streff waited. She could still picture Streff's red beard twitching as he tried not to laugh during those endless meetings. They'd finally found their answer in the DIA's (Defense Intelligence Agency) DX-447- code-named *Shadowseeker*. This was a large, highly classified satellite in geosynchronous orbit around Earth, directly above Nevada's secret "Area 51."

This orbital platform, assembled over many secret space missions, was gigantic. The first time Mandy saw the massive secret satellite, she whispered, "It's like the Death Star had a baby with a greenhouse." The comparison wasn't far off—except this satellite was practically invisible, wrapped in quantum sensors that made it look smaller than her basketball on radar. Its prime equipment and instrumentation bay was a computer geek's dream, and sleek robots that moved in hyper-fast streaks and jerks monitored and attended to its technology. *Shadowseeker's* plexiglass-walled crew area reminded her of those underwater hotels she'd seen on social media, except instead of fish, you watched satellites and space debris drift past.

The weapons bay had made her nervous at first—those twelve "Eagleclaw" missiles looked way too much like her brother's video games coming to life. But the greenhouse... that was something else entirely. Robot gardeners, which somehow managed to be both cool and creepy, tended endless rows of plants under purple growth lights. The air was thick and humid, heavy with the scent of earth and growing things—so different from the sterile atmosphere of the rest of the satellite. She'd watched, fascinated, as they recycled everything from plant condensation to human sweat into fresh water. The classified reactors would impress anyone, splitting water into oxygen for breathing and hydrogen for fuel.

If only she could write her chemistry paper about that instead of electron configurations!

Mandy stretched, yawned, and hurried along softly lit corridors to the CCC. She and her dad stowed their astronaut suits in their lockers. Mandy seconded her dad when he said he would grab a quick shower and added that she would then join her cousins and the rest of the female family members at Grandma's house.

A crudely handwritten sign caught her eye as she approached the elevators: "TELEPORTER IS NOW WORKING" scrawled in black marker on yellow cardboard. Mickey's latest project because, apparently, regular elevators weren't exciting enough. The interlocking tiles set into the floor resembled something out of a retro sci-fi show her dad loved.

"What the heck," Mandy muttered, stepping onto one of the two-foot squares. Her stomach did a little flip as she said, "Third floor." The world blurred, tingled, and snapped back into focus—way faster than the elevators, she had to admit. She found herself on an identical tile on the third floor where the Mandez living quarters were.

"That was actually pretty cool," she said to herself, as Gina's voice cut through her self-congratulation.

"Mandy, oh my gosh! You actually used Mickey's teleporter?" Gina stood a few feet away, wearing a light blue flight suit. Her red shoes squeaked against the polished floor as she hurried over.

"Yeah," Mandy shrugged. "The sign said it was working."

"Well," Gina's eyes widened, "you're the first to try it. Remember when he tried to teleport one of the robot maids? The electronics didn't make the trip—just an empty metal shell standing there!"

"I- feel- fine," Mandy said in her best robot voice, making jerky movements with her arms.

"Except you're about four inches shorter, and your hair is purple now," Gina teased.

"What!?" Mandy's hand flew to her hair. "I'll turn him into a frog!"

"No, no," Gina grabbed her arm, laughing. "I'm kidding! You're still the same beautiful, regular-sized, green-haired, green-skinned woman you've been since you started wearing that amulet. But wow, you lose your temper fast."

Mandy playfully shoved her cousin as they headed toward her bedroom suite. Again, the amulet at her throat felt warm against her skin—a constant reminder of how much her life had changed. "I need a shower. Wait for me so we can go to Grandma's together."

"Sure." Gina flopped onto the dark brown leather sofa, pulling out her silver tablet. "That's why I was waiting. But hurry—I can already smell the lamb meat in Grandma's stew!"

When Mandy exited her bathroom, she found Gina sitting on her bed. Mandy said, "Okay, let me throw together a backpack for Grandma's house, and we'll be out of here."

Gina's hazel eyes twinkled as she asked, "So, how was the Moon?"

Throwing her favorite pink socks into her backpack, Mandy replied, "It was good. Both the Oxy-ginator and Aqua-ginator worked perfectly." Gina said, "I still can't get over how you shrunk that entire building to take to space!"

"Yeaaaaah…" Mandy said slowly and softly, zipping up her backpack. "I need to come clean about that. It really wiped me out for about three days." She sank onto her bed, the memory making her muscles ache all over again.

LUNAR 1 had been like nothing she'd ever done before. NASA had built the basic structure in just four months—a behemoth the size of a football stadium. She remembered walking through it on Earth, her footsteps echoing off wooden beams while construction crews threaded miles of colored cables and plumbing through the framework. The whole thing had looked like a giant's half-finished treehouse.

Then came the hard part. She and Danny had worked together, transforming wood into titanium, section by section. The spell left a metallic taste in her mouth and made her fingers tingle for hours afterward. But watching the dull lumber shimmer and transform into gleaming metal and glass had been worth every headache.

Then Mandy and her dad went to the Moon (on the trip they had just returned from) to activate the Oxy-ginators and Aqua-ginator. These devices were basically magic masquerading as science—taking in carbon dioxide and spitting out pure oxygen through a process that would make her chemistry teacher's head spin. The Aqua-ginators were even cooler, combining hydrogen with leftover oxygen from the Oxy-ginators to create water. Both machines hummed with the extra energy that was a byproduct of their reactions, feeding power into the base's emergency batteries.

"But getting it all to the Moon..." Mandy shook her head, slipping her feet back into her red shoes. That had been the crazy part.

They made their way to the elevator lobby, their shoes silent on the sleek corridor floor. "Um, let's take the elevators," Gina said, eyeing Mickey's teleporter tiles. "I'm still not convinced by his *Star Trek* wannabe invention."

"*¡Dios mío!*" Mandy muttered as she leaned against the wall. "The Moon may be amazing, but it really wipes you out." She'd used every ounce of power from her wand, ring, and amulet to shrink the entire structure to the size of her mom's refrigerator. The spell had felt like trying to compress a mountain into a matchbox; energy crackled around her, causing her hair to stand on end.

The rest should have been simple: three jumps through portals—from Area 51's secret warehouse to the *Shadowseeker*, then to the Moon's surface. The building, now family-fridge-sized, followed through the cargo portal like an oversized package delivery. But expanding it back to full size... Mandy winced at the memory. It felt like her bones were trying to stretch along with the building. She'd completed the task and add the protective force field that kept it hidden from Earth's telescopes, but after that, everything went fuzzy. She'd woken up three days later to find out the NASA astronauts had practically carried her unconscious body back through the portals.

The elevator doors opened to reveal Mandy's dad still in the CCC. He always wore his red-and-black checked LL Bean flannel shirt over his flight suit. The familiar scent of pine from his aftershave mingled with the metallic air of the complex as she gave him a quick hug.

"Ready for some grandma time?" he asked, squeezing her shoulder. Mandy smiled, "Yes! Though I might sleep through the first day of girl time!"

"You've earned it, *Mija*." He kissed the top of her head. "Go have fun."

Mandy and Gina headed for the final portal of the day—this one leading straight to the basement under Grandma's house. As they approached, the air crackled with familiar energy, and Mandy could already smell the rich aroma of the family's favorite coming through. Her stomach growled in response.

As they stepped through the shimmering doorway, Mandy felt the last of the space mission tension leave her shoulders. She thought, *'It's time for a weekend of being a typical teenager!'* Well, as normal as you can be when your family's basement contains a magical gateway to your grandma's house.

The portal flashed, and they were home.

CHAPTER 2

THE GREEN HAND

G RANDMA'S OLD WHITE CLAPBOARD house was a chaotic
scene - women and girls everywhere, moving her back
in from the Complex. Boxes of groceries competed with
voices in the yellow kitchen. The basement door slammed as
Mandy and Gina bounded in from downstairs. Grandma winced
at the sound.

"Well, I'll be! If it isn't my little whirlwind," Grandma
exclaimed, her eyes twinkling. "And Gina, bless your heart for
waiting. You girls stick together tighter than bark on a tree,
don't you?"

Gina hugged Grandma, then said, "Come on, Mandy, let's
unpack our bags in the dormitory." As Mandy followed Gina

towards the stairway, her mom said, "Don't forget to use the spell to change your appearance! We don't want the neighbors to see you like that."

"OK, Mom," Mandy scowled. She liked her new appearance! Even though she was only thirteen, she appeared to be a full-grown woman in some ways. And the green hair and green skin didn't bother her at all.

That said, her new coloring occasionally reminded her of Loganna, the evil witch they battled in Storyworld. But she promised her Mom and the others that she wouldn't make a scene during this weekend, so she transformed her Dragonstone bracelet into her magic wand as she ascended the light blue carpeted staircase and evoked the spell that changed her appearance to everyone looking at her to be that of brown-haired, hazel-eyed, half-Hispanic, thirteen-year-old Mandy Mandez. As she rounded the staircase corner and re-entered the kitchen, her grandma handed her an old-fashioned wooden broom and said with a grin, "Magic or no magic, the floor needs sweeping. Get to it, Girl!"

After helping with a thorough spring cleaning of Grandma's house, Mandy and Gina relaxed in brightly flowered patio chairs on the front porch.

"I still can't get over that. One of the Aqua-ginators turns garbage into water?" Gina said. She sat with a pensive look, shaking her head quickly, her blonde hair sweeping across her hazel eyes. "Nope, no can do! I will not drink that water."

"Oh, Gina," Mandy said with a hint of annoyance. "You wouldn't have to! There's an eight-acre farm inside *LUNAR 1*, you know. The Aqua-inator, which processes materials from the sewer and garbage, irrigates the area. Drinking, cleaning, and cooking water comes from a completely different Aqua-inator system."

"Oh, cool! That's good to know," Gina replied. "I sure wouldn't want to shower in water that..."

"OH, NO!" Mandy cried, her hands flying up instinctively.

Time seemed to slow. The spring air grew thick like honey. A dark blue sedan was barreling down the street. The driver clearly focused on their phone. Across the road, a young girl with blonde pigtails chased her soccer ball, its black and white panels spinning as it bounced toward the curb. The ball hit the edge of the sidewalk and rolled into the street. The girl followed, her bright yellow shirt a flash of color against the gray asphalt.

Mandy's heart hammered. Without thinking, she channeled power through the Lizardstone. Green energy swirled from her hands, wrapping around the girl like a protective cocoon just as the car's tires hit the spot where she would have been. The whoosh of displaced air ruffled the girl's pigtails as the vehicle sped past, its driver oblivious to the near tragedy.

The green energy dissipated, releasing the girl, who stood frozen mid-stride at the street's edge. She blinked, confused, then turned toward the porch. Her eyes widened.

"Mandy," Gina hissed, grabbing her cousin's arm. "Your disguise!"

Mandy looked down at her hands - green as spring leaves. She ducked behind the porch pillar, her heart still racing from the near miss. Across the street, the girl picked up her soccer ball, staring at the porch with her mouth ajar.

"What did she see?" Mandy whispered. Gina smiled and said, "Just wave! Act natural. Who will believe a story about a green lady with magical powers, anyway?" Mandy quickly recast her disguise spell, but her hands were shaking. "That was too close - both the car and being spotted."

The girl clutched her ball tightly, then gave a hesitant wave back. She glanced both ways before hurrying back to her yard.

"You saved her life," Gina whispered. "Sometimes, that's worth the risk."

"Yeah," Mandy agreed, watching the girl disappear into her house. "But Mom will flip if she finds out I lost control of the disguise spell. Again."

The weekend was full of girl talk, cooking, and shopping. Just what one would expect from a group of five women—and six girls, ages nine to thirteen. Finally, on Monday morning, everyone packed up and prepared to return to the Complex and their busy lives as part of the FBI's most secret organization.

Grandma spoke up, "OK, girls! Now, listen here, buttercups. It's been a hoot having you all scampering about, but my bridge club'll be here faster than you can say, Jack Robinson. Best skedaddle before they arrive, or you'll be roped into serving tea and crumpets!"

Laughter ensued all around. Grandma pulled Mandy aside, her weathered hands clasping Mandy's. "Now, sweetheart, remember what I always say: magic is like pepper. Powerful in small doses, but too much'll burn you something fierce. You be careful out there, you hear?"

Mandy nodded, touched by her grandmother's concern. "I will, Grandma. Thanks."

Everyone took turns giving Grandma hugs as they trooped down the gray concrete steps to the basement entrance, where they would pass through the portal into the Dungeon, from which they would return to the Complex. As usual, Mandy was the last to appear from the upstairs dormitory. The doorbell sounded its classic "Ding-Dong" chime as she approached Grandma. Distracted, Mandy gave her grandma a quick hug.

"Oh, my friends must be arriving early," Grandma said. "Goodbye, dear."

As Mandy prepared to close the heavy oak-colored basement door behind her, she heard Grandma answer the door and lingered to listen.

"Hello, can I help you?" Grandma asked.

"Yes, ma'am," a deep male voice with a strange accent said. "My friends and I are looking for a friend of ours. The little girl said she was here. Her name is Lu Long."

Before Grandma could respond, Mandy pushed the basement door open and shouted from the doorway, "Alexa! Intruder Alert!" Immediately, a force barrier, almost transparent, appeared around the house and threw the man from the porch onto the lawn. Mandy ran from the basement stairs and across to the front door, slammed it shut, and turned just in time to see Grandma magically teleported away. In a flash, Mandy turned her Dragonstone cuff bracelet into her magic wand and peered through the bright red gingham drapes that decorated the front windows to see what was happening. As she did this, she reflexively plugged her magic earbud into her right ear.

"Mandy!" came Uncle Tyler's voice over the earbud. "What's going on?"

"I'm not sure yet," Mandy replied. "Did everyone get back to the Complex safely?"

"Yes," Uncle Tyler said. "The new voice-activated security system you and I installed in the house worked perfectly. And that teleporting spell you put on Grandma's wedding ring worked like a charm!" he chuckled. "It got her here in an instant. Everyone else has come through the portal, Mandy. You should do the same!"

"Not yet," Mandy replied. "I need to look into this. Make sure the outside cameras are working, OK?"

"I'm on it!" Uncle Tyler confirmed.

Mandy looked through the drapes again. Two black SUVs with darkly tinted windows sat in front of the house. Two men helped the man who had fallen off the porch to his feet. All three were each well over six feet tall with military-precise haircuts and matching dark mustaches. Their navy-blue suit jackets couldn't quite conceal the distinctive shape of Glock 17s in tactical holsters. Their synchronized, professional movements suggested special forces training.

A fourth man appeared from the lead SUV—a midnight-black Cadillac Escalade with diplomatic plates. The vehicle's door swung open with a soft hydraulic hiss, and a man unfolded his six-foot-four frame from the dark leather interior. His tan Armani suit, perfectly tailored to his broad shoulders, caught the morning light as he surveyed the house. A light blue Thomas Pink shirt stretched across his chest, and Italian leather loafers clicked deliberately against the pavement as he took a step forward.

Then, Mandy noticed a sizeable beaded bracelet on his thick left wrist. It contained a glowing green Lizardstone. The stone's power had transformed his entire left hand, turning the skin a vibrant emerald that contrasted with the ebony complexion of his face. He was loud, giving orders to his team.

"He's a wizard!" cried Mandy. "And they said that Lu Long was their friend."

Mandy immediately waved her wand around herself. A blink later, she appeared in the Complex Command Center and dashed across the polished floor to join her family. An FDM team was there, too. They had gathered rapidly in response to the alarm raised by the intruder alert. Everyone present studied the wall of glowing monitors displaying live feeds from the security cameras mounted around her Grandma's home.

A red-haired female FDM team member, wearing a white lab coat and a pink blouse, reached forward to tap a switch on a monitor. Instantly, the voice of the man with the bracelet back at Grandma's house echoed through the room. His voice carried the crisp accent of someone who had learned English at an expensive private school. "I detected your magic a few days ago, Lu Long," he said, his voice edged with barely controlled rage. "Your signature was unmistakable. The weapons you promised were due weeks ago. Have you ..." He paused, the Lizardstone flaring brighter with his anger, "...betrayed me?"

He raised his left hand. Mandy watched as emerald energy crackled between his fingers. Emerald energy now danced openly across his transformed hand, casting shifting shadows across his angular features. "My organization paid $2 billion for those weapons. And I resent betrayal."

Through her earbud, Uncle Tyler's voice carried a measured urgency. "Mandy, this situation has taken on a life of its own and is now moving at full speed. Lu Long wasn't just dabbling— she was perfecting something dangerous. This is a bigger mess than a dragon in a porcelain shop. Our intelligence suggests Lu Long was working to enhance magical artifacts using quantum technology. The plans were supposed to be included with the missiles."

Mandy unconsciously touched the amulet at her throat. Lu Long's amulet. The one that mushroomed her powers when combined with her Dragonstone wand. Was that what he was looking for?

"My patience," the fourth man's voice dropped to a dangerous whisper that somehow carried more menace than his previous shouting had, "...is at an end. I've tracked magical signatures across four continents in search of Lu Long." His transformed hand clenched into a fist, green energy crackling between his knuckles. "Now I find this house practically glowing with enchantments." Each word fell like ice: "*Where... is... she?*"

Then, something down the street caught his attention. A predatory smile spread across his features as he turned to his men, snapping orders in a language Mandy didn't recognize. The men moved with military precision back to their vehicles— but before they could pull away, a champagne-colored Toyota Camry parked behind the SUVs.

Mrs. Sparks stepped out, resplendent in her raspberry-colored dress and pristine white loafers. Her heels clicked cheerfully against the sidewalk as she balanced a crystal plate piled with dainty cucumber sandwiches. Her silver hair caught the morning sun as she started up the porch steps, utterly unaware of the danger.

"Mom!" Agent Sparks's cry echoed through the Command Center, raw with horror. The room erupted into chaos. Agent Sparks lunged for the portal controls. Two other agents caught her arm to restrain her.

"Protocol!" Agent Chen shouted over the commotion, his usual calm demeanor cracking. "We can't risk—"

"That's my mother out there!" Agent Sparks fought against her colleagues' restraining grip. Her face had blanched, eyes fixed on the monitor. Before anyone could react, two of the thugs exploded from the nearest SUV.

"Well, I'll be buttered on both sides," Mrs. Sparks said as the thugs approached. "You boys look like you're in quite a hurry! Care for a sandwich before you go about your business?"

Neither thug spoke. Their movements were fluid and practiced—one seized Mrs. Sparks from behind while the other clamped a massive hand over her mouth. The crystal plate spun out of her grasp, sandwiches scattering across the lawn like fallen leaves. They dragged her toward the vehicle, her white loafers scraping helplessly against the concrete. The Command Center fell silent instantly. Agent Sparks stopped struggling, her shoulders sagging, her fists clenched. "Mom..." she sobbed.

Mandy didn't wait to hear more. Power surged through her as she teleported to her grandmother's porch in a flash of green light—but she was seconds too late. The SUVs' engines roared as they sped down the street. Mrs. Sparks's wide, terrified eyes met Mandy's through the tinted window just before the vehicles vanished into a shimmering emerald portal that split the air like a wound. The portal snapped shut with a thunderclap, leaving only the scent of ozone and scattered sandwiches on the lawn.

Then the wizard's voice invaded Mandy's mind, smooth as silk but sharp as steel: "So! You hold Lu Long's amulet! Very well. I'll trade you this sweet old lady for it. Meet me tomorrow at this time for the exchange."

"Who are you?" Mandy demanded aloud, her voice shaking with rage. "Where will I find you?"

"I am Kijani M'kono." The voice now held a hint of amusement. "They call me Green Hand! Find me in... the Sahara." A pause. "Come alone if you value this woman's life."

The connection broke, leaving Mandy on the porch, fists clenched, staring at the empty street where Mrs. Sparks had vanished. Behind her, the security barrier shimmered like a soap bubble in the morning sun, protecting a house that suddenly felt much less safe.

CHAPTER 3

HOSTAGE NEGOTIATIONS

AGENT SPARKS'S BOOTS ECHOED across the Command Center floor as she stormed toward Mandy. "Oz! Why didn't you stop them? They took my Mother!"

"I...I..." Mandy shook her head, her mind drawing a complete blank on how to respond to this situation.

Turning to the rest of the room, Agent Sparks said, "What are we going to do now?" Then she turned and pointed her finger at Mandy. "This is all your fault! What were those guys even doing at your Grandma's house? I'm betting you were showing off with your magical amulet ... they detected its magic

... and traced you to that house! And then you ran away back here — while my mother gets kidnapped!"

"Gail! Stop this right now!" Mandy's mom shouted, her brown eyes flashing.

"Gail, I know you're upset about your mother being kidnapped. I get that. But," and her voice softened, "you ... are ... not ... thinking ... clearly. This isn't Mandy's fault, and no, I'm not just saying that as her mom. Think! There's no way she—or anyone—could have expected this would happen. So, let's all catch our breath and give her a chance to talk."

"Mom, no. She's right," Mandy breathed. "I used my amulet magic."

Gina joined in, "Wait! Wait—you did that to save the little girl across the street. The girl ran into the street after a ball and almost got hit by a car.

"That doesn't matter," Mandy said, shaking her head. "No. The wizard was there because he thought Lu Long was there! He told me telepathically that he would trade Mrs. Sparks for the amulet tomorrow. I'm supposed to find him somewhere in the Sahara Desert, and I'm supposed to come alone."

Agent Sparks collapsed into a leather armchair with a heavy sigh, the weight of her mother's kidnapping pulling her shoulders down. "So let me get this right. You're saying he said that you meet with him in the Sahara freaking desert, give him your amulet, and he gives you *my mother*?"

Mickey quickly shook his head "No," and said, "No, no, no! I don't think it will work that way at all. I'll bet my bottom dollar that once a Lizardstone bonds with you, it bonds for life!"

The others in the room looked at Mickey for an explanation. "Don't you see? This wizard intends to kill Oz!" he blurted.

"OK, hang on, Mickey. That will not happen," Mandy said with renewed confidence. "We have twenty-four hours to devise a plan to save Mrs. Sparks. I need some time to think. Let's all gather back here in an hour, OK?

"Oh, and by the way, the wizard called himself 'Green Hand.' I'm not sure why I think this way, but I'm feeling that he's been behind everything we've been fighting for the past year!"

An hour later, the M-Force assembled in the dimly lit Command Center. Agent Sparks and six FDM commandos joined them, the somber mood heavy in the air. She held up her hand for silence.

"Before we start," Agent Sparks said, her voice tight with control, "I want to apologize for earlier. The protocol states that I need to step back from this operation." She gestured to Agent Conners. "He'll lead the FBI's involvement."

"Wait." Mandy stepped forward. "The FDM can't be involved. This wizard's magic..." She shuddered. "Even I got spooked when I sensed his power. But I have a plan."

Agent Sparks studied her boots before giving a curt nod. "Let's hear it."

Mandy laid out her strategy, mapping each team member's role and responsibilities. The plan was bold, maybe even crazy, but it might work if they could coordinate the timing perfectly.

"Hold on," Agent Blackman interrupted. "Green Hand is expecting this showdown. He'll have fail-safes on Mrs. Sparks - probably magical booby traps to force you into a real fight."

Mandy turned to J.T. "Could you scan her and disable any traps while I keep him distracted?" J.T.'s eyes narrowed thoughtfully. "Yes, Miss Oz. If I'm close enough."

"Then you're with us," Mandy said. Let's review it one more time. Everyone needs to know their part cold."

They drilled the plan until exhaustion set in. At midnight, Mandy finally called it. *"Descansen bien,"* she said, her voice firm. "At 10:00 AM tomorrow, we face him in the Sahara."

As the team filed out, Agent Sparks caught Mandy's sleeve and spoke softly, "Oz, bring my mother home, please."

"I will," Mandy promised. "Whatever it takes." Left alone in the Command Center, Mandy slumped into a chair. Only then, in the darkness, did she let the tears come.

At nine the following morning, the team, comprising Mandy and her mom, Uncle Tyler, Mickey, Gina, Jenny, and the twins, Mary and Jane, all showed up in the courtyard. A few minutes later, J.T. arrived as well.

"Guys," Mandy said aloud over the earbud comms, "are you in place in the CCC to monitor?"

"All in place," Agent Blackman replied.

"Doc," Mandy said again, "is the infirmary on alert?"

"I'm all set, Mandy," Aunt Kate replied. "Oh, Oz. Sorry. I'm still not used to this codename lingo."

"It's OK, Doc," replied Mandy. She turned to the twins and said, "Girls, we need Gemini."

Mary's fingers intertwined with Jane's, their twin faces mirroring identical looks of concentration. The air crackled, then exploded with an orange flame that whirled around them like a cyclone. When the fire dissipated, Gemini stood in their place - a massive saber-toothed tiger with gleaming wings and two powerful heads, each sporting long fangs that glinted in the morning light.

Mary said, "Ready and waiting."

Jane said, "Anticipating."

Gemini (both heads in unison): "Our claws are sharp, our wings unfurled. Say the word, Oz, and we'll take on the world!" Their merged voice rumbled like distant thunder, a low purr underlying the words.

Mandy then turned to Jenny. "Your turn, Prism."

Jenny adjusted her stance, her hands forming intricate symbols, as they always did when she was about to speak. With her trademark lisp and all, her voice resonated with crystalline clarity, carrying an almost musical cadence as she cast the spell that would transform Dragonstone into a wand. But in a rainbow-colored flash, it transformed her into a walking, multi-faceted jewel.

Prism hopped up onto Gemini's back and sat behind its right head. Then, J.T. hopped up behind Gemini's left head.

Mandy nodded approval. Then she looked at Gina and asked, "Have you located them yet?"

"No, darn it!" Gina sighed. "I've been scanning all over the Sahara, but I haven't found him yet. I think he must be using some sort of cloaking device."

Mandy considered that for a full minute. "Well, hang in there with your search. He'll have to make himself visible. Otherwise, how would he expect me to find him?"

Gina nodded. Her hazel eyes narrowed as she continued to scan across the Atlantic Ocean, over Africa, and into the Sahara Desert. Her mind searched for any sign of Green Hand's location.

Then, exactly one minute before ten, she exclaimed, "There! A green beacon just flared to life! The wizard's there with Mrs. Sparks - she's tied to a chair inside some kind of energy field. She looks pretty scared."

Mandy heard Agent Sparks whisper, "Oh, Mom, hang in there!" in her earbuds and stopped momentarily to collect her thoughts. Then she said, "Prism, put a spell around yourself and Gemini. Gemini, when you see my blue portal, fly through it, but stay up high until you see that I've got Green Hand distracted."

Prism's form shimmered, refracting light in a dazzling array as she raised her arms. Her voice, like the chime of glass in the wind, carried the spell across the team. "In shadows, we now reside, cloaked in the unseen tide. Bind this spell, with light denied!" The magic flowed over her, J.T., and Gemini, wrapping them in an iridescent veil until they vanished altogether.

"OK, guys," Mandy said softly, "Let's do this!" Mandy formed a blue energy ball around her mom, Mickey, and Uncle Tyler, cloaking the three from sight. Then, she formed a green energy ball around herself and them and transported them to the location Gina had identified in the Sahara.

The desert sun stabbed her eyes. Through the heat shimmer, Green Hand stood waiting—an imposing figure in white harem pants, his ebony skin gleaming, his Lizardstone bracelet pulsating with deadly power.

The hood of Mandy's poncho was up and in place, and the Cocoon spell shielded her face from his view. Her left hand remained hidden in her sleeve to hide her Lizardstone ring. The green energy field cloaking her and her companions glowed from her Lizardstone amulet. She raised her wand, took a defensive stance, and pointed her wand toward the sky. She twirled it slightly, hoping Green Hand wouldn't notice the blue portal in the sky above them.

"Ah, witch!" Green Hand snarled, his emerald energy crackling, "Hand over the amulet!" Mrs. Sparks, seated nearby with her hands bound, arched an eyebrow.

Mandy worked hard to keep her voice calm, unemotional, and expressionless. "I don't think so, Green Hand. You know I can't just hand it over to you," Mandy said, listening to J.T. in her earbuds as he told her he and his group were in place and ready.

"Well, yes," he replied, chuckling, "I knew that! But I didn't know if you did!"

In one swift motion, he raised his left arm and closed its hand into a fist. With that motion, twenty men holding diamond-tipped spears appeared around her. "Excellent!" he hissed. Then he opened and closed his hand again — and ten men, just like the others, surrounded Delores Sparks.

With a mock laugh, Mandy said, "Spears? Oooh, I'm so afraid."

Green Hand bowed his head, roared in laughter, and said, "Kill her!" Each warrior surrounding Mandy immediately thrust his spear toward her, and a green bolt of energy shot out of it! While Mandy's force field held, she felt a vicious burning pain. She groaned deeply.

"Mandy!" her mom cried over the earbuds. "Let us out of the energy field to help you fight back!"

"Not...yet," Mandy whispered. "J.T., you need to move fast and get Mrs. Sparks! I can't hold this for long!" Taking a deep breath and closing her eyes momentarily to gather her magic, Mandy freed her left hand from its sleeve and shot energy bolts out at the warriors. She aimed from her front to her left, disabling all the warriors to her left.

Green Hand started at Mandy's hand. "You have the ring? No!" he bellowed. "Kill her!" he commanded again. He joined his warriors by shooting energy bolts from his now trembling hand. Looking towards the men guarding Mrs. Sparks, he said, "The rest of you, join us! I must have those Lizardstones!" The five men surrounding Mrs. Sparks ran over, replaced the fallen warriors, and joined the attack.

With this new onslaught of energy bolts, Mandy screamed again and fell to her knees. Her mother's scream of "Mandy!" filled her earbuds.

"Not... yet, not yet!" Mandy groaned between whimpering screams. Again, she gathered her magic and shot more green energy bolts from her left hand, disabling more warriors. J.T.'s voice broke through her screams, "Mandy, we have her! We have her! She's safe. Get out of there now!"

Mandy stood and raised her wand to the sky, making a broad circular motion. Green Hand looked up, then quickly glanced over and saw that Mrs. Sparks was nowhere to be seen. His anger erupted in a deafening yell, and he wildly shot energy bolts into the sky towards the blue portal! A burst of sizzling white light instantly blinded him in return.

Good one, Prism, Mandy thought as she removed the cloaking shield from around the others. Simultaneously, bolts of purple, yellow, and silver energy shot from Mandy, incapacitating the rest of the warriors as they writhed on the scorching desert sands. Green Hand was taken aback by these events. He instinctively conjured a protective shield around himself as he watched three cloaked figures materialize beside Mandy, their wands blazing with power! Moving slowly and painfully, Mandy stood up and joined the others, each assaulting Green Hand with glowing energy bolts. Seeing no chance to win or get his prize, Green Hand crossed his arms and vanished from the desert sands, taking his fallen warriors with him.

Mandy fell to her knees, and her head drooped for a moment. Then, gathering herself, she whispered a spell. The desert heat vanished as they materialized out of the Sahara.

CHAPTER 4

WARBIRD

"MANDY, THIS ISN'T—" MICKEY'S urgent voice cut through the darkness. "The transport failed. Where are we?"

The sharp tang of salt air and diesel fuel burned Mandy's nostrils as she lay on the rough asphalt, still warm from the day's heat. Above them, flickering yellow security lights cast long shadows across the dock, and machinery clanged against metal containers somewhere in the distance. Mandy's protective force field shimmered around them like a soap bubble in the dim light.

"Mickey," Mandy's mom asked, bending down to her daughter, "can you teleport out of her energy ball?" Mickey replied, "I think so." He raised his wand but stopped when he felt someone grab his ankle.

"No," Mandy rasped, her throat raw from the battle in the desert. "No magic. He...might...find...us. If he does..." She swallowed hard. "...I'm not sure we can beat him."

The metallic clang of a crane echoed across the water as Uncle Tyler whispered, "Mandy's shield must be cloaking us! Two men just walked by and didn't even look our way."

Mandy's mom touched her earpiece. "Command, are you there?"

"Affirmative. We hear you," came the reply, crackling with static.

"It looks like we're at a shipyard or a port." Mandy's mom continued. The salt breeze tugged at her auburn hair. "I'm not sure where. Mandy, do you know where you took us?"

"Nor... North." Each word sent fresh waves of pain through Mandy's battered body. "It hurts so bad, Mom. I need Gina." Mandy's mom raised her voice, "Gina! Can you see us?"

"Not if you're cloaked," Gina replied. "Try to figure out where you are. Can you find a landmark or something I can use to locate you?

Uncle Tyler and Mickey stood within Mandy's energy ball, scanning all directions. The night air grew colder, carrying the musty scent of canvas from nearby ships.

"Gina," Uncle Tyler spoke up, his breath visible in the cooling air, "I see a cruise ship to the east. Based on the Arabic writing on that building, I think we're in Alexandria, Egypt. Look for a Holland Cruise Line ship in the port!"

The group waited in tense silence, broken only by the rhythmic slap of waves against the dock pilings and distant shouts in Arabic from the night shift workers. The force field hummed faintly around them, a constant reminder of their precarious safety. After a brief interval, Gina confirmed she had Alexandria in her magical sight and described the same cruise ship. The discussion turned to extraction plans, voices kept low as dock workers passed nearby, their boots scraping against the rough pavement.

Finally, Mickey's voice cut through the whispered debate. "Warbird!" He repeated the name three more times, each shout echoing across the water. Agent Sparks' voice crackled through their earbuds, "Of course! Warbird! Hold on, everyone! Give me a few minutes."

Mandy shifted against the warm asphalt, trying to find a position that didn't send shooting pains through her body. She remembered the ships they'd captured from Lu Long—*the Green Jade* and the *Green Jade II*. Both vessels had been transformed from simple cargo ships into sophisticated FDM vessels, though they maintained their ordinary exterior.

Hidden in their holds were batteries of surface-to-air missiles, torpedoes, and three drone aircraft. Each ship also concealed a modified Navy Apache attack helicopter. To any observer, they appeared to be generic cargo vessels - their lethal capabilities were invisible to prying eyes.

The late-night air grew colder as they waited. Mandy could smell the mixture of engine oil and rust mingled with the ever-present salt breeze. Her mom's poncho, tucked under her head, did little to cushion her against the hard ground.

"That was good thinking, Bamf," Agent Sparks announced after a five-minute silence. "We stationed Warbird 1 in the Mediterranean Sea. From its location, it can be there in ten hours."

Mandy's mom looked at Mandy and received a thumbs up. She said, "Mandy's a go on that, Command. We'll wait here undercover. When *Warbird 1* nears port, patch them in, and we'll figure out how to get on board."

The night settled around them, broken only by the distant thrum of ship engines and the inevitable, occasional shouting of dock workers. The asphalt had long since lost its warmth, leaving them all shivering slightly in the Mediterranean night air.

Through the haze of pain, Mandy couldn't help but smile, thinking about Mickey's quick thinking. She remembered how he'd come up with the name 'Warbird' after Prism enchanted the ships with her invisibility spell, insisting it was just like a Klingon warbird from *Star Trek*. Now she noticed him trying to hide a slight blush in the dim security lights, and she knew exactly why - Commander Khammy Pakiko. The memory of Mickey's first glimpse of the Commander at the Complex swimming pool was still fresh - the Hawaiian officer, with her flowing ebony hair and curvy, athletic build, had stopped Mickey dead in his tracks. He'd followed her around like a lovesick puppy ever since, and she'd been kind enough to let him officially christen the ship as "*Warbird 1*," complete with a champagne bottle ceremony. Mandy noticed Mickey was smiling to himself! And even blushing a little. She thought, *He sure has a crush on the captain of Warbird 1!*

Mandy could tell he was already thinking about seeing Commander Pakiko again, and she usually would have teased him about it, but the brutal pain of her injuries spoiled the mood. *Maybe later*, Mandy thought. Usually, Mandy would have teased him mercilessly, but right now, each breath sent sharp pains through her chest. The metallic taste of the magical battle still lingered in her mouth, mixing unpleasantly with the briny air.

"Get some rest, honey," her mom whispered, carefully adjusting the folded poncho under Mandy's head. The rough canvas scratched her cheek, but she was too exhausted to notice.

Uncle Tyler stretched, his joints cracking in the quiet night. "I'll take the first watch. The rest of you try to sleep. I'll wake you in three hours."

Mandy closed her eyes, but sleep proved elusive. The cold of the asphalt seeped through her clothes, and every slight movement sent fresh waves of pain through her body. *If only Gina were here*, she thought. *Gina's healing touch could ease this agony. But then what?* The memory of Green Hand's power made her shudder - the raw energy that had crackled from his transformed hand was more intense than anything she'd faced before. Maybe even stronger than Loganna.

She forced those thoughts away, focusing instead on their escape plan. Once aboard *Warbird 1*, they could use the portal system she'd helped design. She could almost picture the two permanent portals—the large cargo hold portal connecting to the FDM base outside D.C. and the personnel portal behind the bridge. The familiar scent of ozone that accompanied each transport seemed preferable to this cold dock with its mix of diesel fumes and sea spray. The gentle lapping of waves against the dock eventually lulled her into an uneasy sleep.

Mickey's finger jabbing into her shoulder jolted her awake. "Mandy," he whispered, "*Warbird 1* is docking. About a mile down. Think you can walk?"

Through heavy eyelids, she could see the sky had lightened to pre-dawn gray. The massive silhouette of a cargo ship was barely visible in the distance, its engines sending low vibrations through the dock. She tried to stand, but white-hot pain shot through her back, forcing her down with a grimace.

"I can't," she managed through clenched teeth. "Can't stand." Uncle Tyler started to lift her, but even that gentle movement drew a moan of pain. Mandy's mom's face tightened with concern, her deep blue eyes registering concern for her child. She touched her earpiece. "Command, this is Cash."

The static-filled reply came immediately: "Go ahead, Cash."

"Have Spyglass transport directly to *Warbird 1* and meet us on deck. Make sure the Captain has the energy field activated." Her mom's voice held an edge of urgency that made Mandy's stomach tighten. "Alert us when Spyglass is on board."

"Wilco, we're on it."

Steam whistled from the distant ship's vents as it secured its moorings—the sound of heavy chains and metal groaning carried across the water. Mandy's mom turned to Mickey, whose face had gone slightly pale in the growing light.

"Bamf, you need to teleport Oz to the ship. The energy field will let you out, and the ship's field will let you through." Mickey's voice shook. "I've never teleported with someone else. What if ..."

"Do it, Mickey!" The sharp tone in her mom's voice made them all flinch. "Mandy's in too much pain. You're her only chance." Mickey nodded slowly, eyes downcast. Then he looked up. "But wait - what about you and Uncle Tyler?" Her mom's tight grin didn't reach her eyes. "It's three AM. Ain't nobody here! We'll just... walk to the ship and up the gangplank!"

The grin vanished as a woman's crisp and professional voice came through their earbuds: "Cash, this is *Warbird 1*. Everything is in place. Ready for you to come aboard."

Mickey knelt beside Mandy, his arm sliding carefully under her head. The others pulled up their hoods; the Cocoon spell shimmering around their faces. Despite the pain, Mandy couldn't resist one last whisper: "You're gonna see *Mo-an-a!*"

"Shut up," Mickey muttered, but his ears reddened. He took a deep breath, squeezing his eyes shut in a state of intense concentration. "I hope this works!"

The world twisted sideways in a rush of vertigo. When it settled, the smell of salt air was more pungent, mingling with the scents of fresh paint and metal. The deck of *Warbird 1* felt solid beneath them, though it rolled slightly with the harbor swells. Gina's footsteps pounded across the deck. She dropped to her knees beside them as Mickey gently lowered Mandy. The cool touch of Gina's hand against Mandy's skin brought immediate relief, but she could feel her cousin's body tensing as she drew out the pain and injury. Five minutes later, Gina collapsed beside her, both of them unconscious under the watercolor sky.

The sharp antiseptic smell roused Mandy from unconsciousness; then she opened her eyes. The soft, rhythmic beeping of medical monitors filled the air, and crisp sheets rustled as she shifted in the hospital bed. The familiar light green walls and tan floors of the Complex infirmary came into focus. To her left, Gina lay motionless in another bed, the gentle rise and fall of her chest the only movement.

"How are you feeling, honey?" Her mom's voice drew her attention. Mandy tried to sit up, her muscles protesting every movement. The metallic taste of the magical battle still lingered in her mouth. "I'll get by, gracias Mamá. How long have we been here?"

"Two days." Her mom's voice was soft, barely louder than the humming machines. "Your Uncle Tyler carried you both through the portal. Dr. Kate says Gina will be okay." She paused, lips pursed. "But it's taking time for her to regain her strength."

"What about the Warbird?" The words felt rough in Mandy's throat.

"It remained in Alexandria until today, maintaining appearances." Her mom settled into the chair beside the bed, the vinyl squeaking slightly. "Loading cargo that Agent Sparks arranged, making it look routine. It's back at sea, in stealth mode, patrolling until needed."

"And Mrs. Sparks?"

"She's just fine," Mandy's mom reassured. "Apparently, she had a delightful chat with one guard about the importance of composting. Gail says she's sworn to secrecy—after insisting they let her make tea for everyone first." A small smile crossed her mom's face. It takes some adjustments to learn that your neighbors are witches. But she's sworn to secrecy. She and Grandma will stay here until we handle the Green Hand situation."

The memory of his power made Mandy's skin crawl. Her head dropped, the starched pillowcase crinkling beneath it. "I'm not sure if we can beat him. He's so strong, Mom!" Her voice cracked. "And he wants my Lizardstones. He'll kill anyone. Mom, I won't kid you. I'm terrified."

"I know, Mandy." Her mom's hand was warm on her arm. "But we have to do what we have to do. I can't imagine what he'd do to the world with more Lizardstone power." She straightened, changing the subject. "Agent Sparks wants us to devise a plan once you and Gina have recovered. She's in D.C. now, briefing the President."

Mandy swung her legs over the side of the bed, ignoring the lingering ache in her muscles. The antiseptic smell suddenly reminded her of how long it'd been since she'd eaten. "I'm hungry. Think Cook can fix me something delicious?" The familiar scents of the cafeteria were already calling to her, promising comfort food and a momentary escape from the weight of what lay ahead.

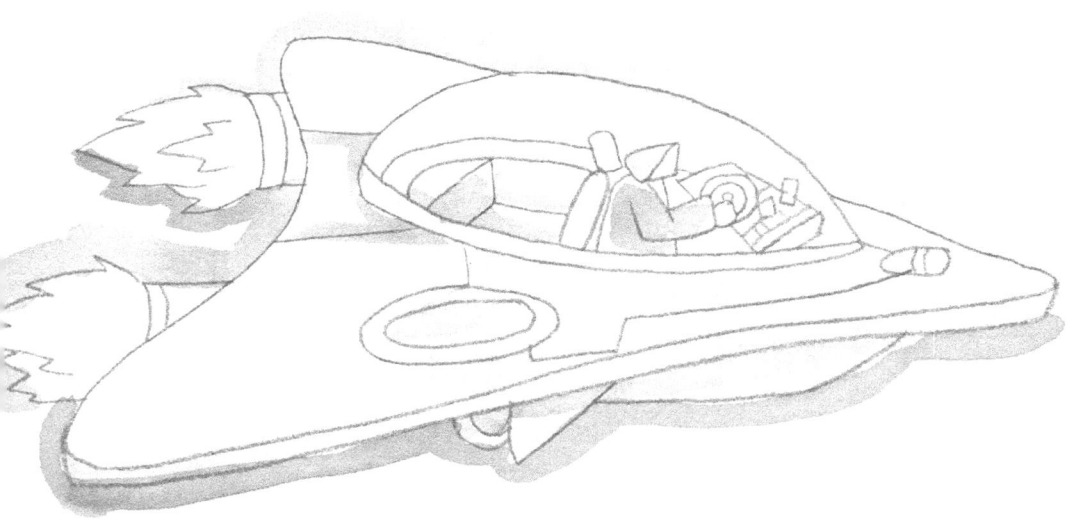

CHAPTER 5

HUMMINGBIRD

TWO DAYS LATER, MANDY and Gina emerged from the elevator, their footsteps echoing in the chrome hallway. Mandy winced slightly as she walked, her muscles still protesting from the battle in the desert. The familiar scent of coffee and electronics that permeated the Complex did little to lift her fatigue.

"Where's Mickey?" Mandy asked, rubbing her sore shoulder. "I haven't seen him since the Sahara, and I wanted to thank him for teleporting me to the *Warbird.*"

"I think he's avoiding us!" Gina said conspiratorially from behind a wide grin. "I think he's afraid we'll tease him about Moana." Mandy chuckled at that as they entered the briefing area. "Yeah, you're probably right. But I *don't* see him. Hey, wait, I don't see *any* of the guys!"

The oak chairs scattered throughout the room sat empty, the afternoon light from the overhead panels reflecting off their polished surfaces. Mickey and Danny's usual spots were vacant. So were her dad's chair and all of her uncles!

Something's wrong, Mandy thought. *This meeting was crucial - they needed to devise a plan against Green Hand.* Just thinking about him sent an involuntary shiver down her spine, the memory of the desert pain still fresh. Mandy motioned to Gina, and they eased into two chairs, the leather creaking softly. The room's cool air conditioning raised goosebumps on Mandy's arms as Agent Sparks strode in, her boots clicking against the polished floor.

"We need to postpone this meeting a few more days," Agent Sparks announced, her voice tight with frustration. I've been called back to Washington to meet with the Department of Homeland Security. Keep thinking about what our plans should be. I'll be back as soon as I can."

Geez, political bureaucracy, Mandy thought with a mental eye roll.

Carefully pushing herself up from her chair, Mandy made her way to where her mom and aunts clustered near the window. "Hey, where are all the guys? None of them came to this meeting, and I haven't seen Mickey or my dad for days."

Aunt Laina brushed her long brown bangs away from her pale green eyes. "They've been working on something in the shop. Mickey said it's top secret and won't say a word about the fool thing, whatever it is!"

"Uh-oh." Gina grabbed Mandy's arm. "C'mon, let's find out what they're up to."

What's going on, Mandy thought. *This is important. We don't have time to mess around. We need to devise a plan to combat Green Hand.*

They moved with purpose, their post-battle stiffness clear in their cautious movements. The maintenance building stood silent, its doors locked and windows wholly obscured.

"Can you see inside?" Mandy whispered. Gina shook her head. "I can't see magically because something is blocking my sight." Mandy tried to transport through the walls with a wave of her wand, but she couldn't penetrate the force field surrounding the entire building. Just as frustration set in, a door opened. The duo ducked behind a lawn tractor and watched as J.T. emerged, followed by Mandy's dad, Uncle Tyler, Uncle Mike, Danny, and Joey. A cargo door slid open beside them, revealing something extraordinary. A sleek, burgundy-colored vehicle hovered silently at eye level. It looked like a hybrid between a spaceship and a fairground ride—a long, pointed front, stubby wings, and a jet engine at the rear. The craft glowed with a mesmerizing burgundy-purple hue, completely silent despite its obvious power. And sitting inside was ... *Mickey!*

Uncle Tyler adjusted his visor with a wry smile. "Alright, Mickey, time to test those fancy maneuvers you've been bragging about. J.T., keep an eye out—we don't need this turning into a Hummingbird piñata."

In response, Mickey pulled the visor down on what Mandy thought of as a fighter pilot's helmet.

Mandy could see evidence of a magical force field surrounding the ship, and she watched in stunned amazement as the ship shot high into the air at remarkable speed. Mickey flew his machine in all directions at even faster speeds — even backward! Gina poked Mandy and motioned for her to put in her earbuds. Mandy did, but she couldn't hear anything. Then Gina tapped Mandy's ear with her wand, and suddenly, Mandy could listen to radio chatter between the guys and Mickey. Gina whispered, "They're using a different frequency than normal. Probably so the Complex can't hear them. Boys! They think they're so clever!"

Mandy smiled knowingly as she watched Mickey having the time of his life, zipping here and there in the air. She knew it bugged Mickey that she could transport herself by her energy ball while he was stuck being a passenger.

Uncle Tyler's voice crackled over the comms. "Ok, Mickey, I'll levitate multiple cement blocks into the air. See if you can shoot them down." Uncle Tyler flicked his wand, sending two cement blocks into the air with the precision of a seasoned technician. With another twist, the blocks spun wildly in opposing directions. "Alright, Mickey, let's see if your aim's as good as your ego."

Mickey's ship banked hard, zeroing in on one block. Mandy watched a purple energy bolt leap from the aircraft's front shaft. The first shot missed as Uncle Tyler made the target veer to the left. As Mickey sped past the other target, his ship turned and flew sideways while firing another energy bolt and blasting the cement block to pieces. Uncle Tyler waved his wand again, sending the other block even higher and faster. "Wait! Where is Mickey? I don't see him!" Danny cried out. Suddenly, a purple energy bolt came out of nowhere and destroyed the target, enhancing the smell of burnt sand. Then, just as suddenly, the ship appeared, hovering just above the circle of men, then floated to the ground.

"Looks like the weaponry works just fine when in stealth mode," Mickey said with evident pride as he exited the ship. "I'll take it back into the shop now. Tomorrow, we do speed tests!"

J.T. let out a low whistle. "Not bad for a test run, Bamf. But let's hope those aim-assist features are as good in an actual fight. No offense, but your precision under pressure isn't exactly legendary."

Uncle Tyler stepped forward, rubbing a smudge of grease from his hand onto his sleeve. "Listen up! These Hummingbirds might look shiny and sleek, but remember—they're tools, not magic carpets. Use your head, stick to the plan, and for heaven's sake, try nothing you haven't practiced at least twice." He paused, smirking. "Except you, Mickey. We all know you'll freestyle, anyway."

Murmuring various versions of "Can do," "OK," and "Yes, sir," the guys hurried in behind the ship, high-fiving each other on their way into the workshop building. The doors clicked shut simultaneously behind them.

Gina, still whispering, said, "Well, now we know what the guys were doing when we were at Grandma's." Shaking her head in disbelief, Mandy said, "Yeah, looks like they were having fun! Anyway, let's get back before they spot us. And I think we should let them keep their little secret until they're ready to share it."

Two days later, Agent Sparks returned from Washington, D.C., her frustration palpable as she scheduled a meeting to discuss the Green Hand threat. When Mandy arrived, she immediately noticed the absence of all the male team members. J.T. suddenly appeared in the briefing area, interrupting Agent Sparks' mounting irritation. "Everyone, meet us in the courtyard," he announced.

"This better be good," Agent Sparks muttered, slamming her notebook shut with a muted crack.

The female M-Force members and FDM staff filed into the courtyard, where the missing men stood in a crisp, synchronized line. Three covered objects waited behind them. With a choreographed precision that spoke of countless rehearsals, Uncle Tyler, Mickey, and Danny each took position beside a tarp. In a single, dramatic motion, they pulled away the coverings to reveal three identical burgundy spacecraft. The pilots donned matching helmets and slipped into their vessels. With a practiced flick, they transformed their Dragonstone amulets into wands, inserting them into the control panels. The ships shimmered, each taking on the unique glow of its pilot's Dragonstone—a mesmerizing display of magical technology.

Silence fell as the ships lifted, defying gravity with impossible grace. They zipped and zagged across the sky in a breathtaking aerial ballet. Uncle Tyler's ship hovered motionless while Mickey circled him tightly, and Danny arced overhead in a perfect loop. The finale came swiftly. The three ships rocketed upward, firing energy bolts at the Complex's force field, and then disappeared. A beat of stunned silence followed before everyone erupted in excited chatter. "Where did they go?" Aunt Laina gasped. "They just... vanished!"

A moment later, the ships reappeared precisely where they'd started; the pilots stepping out to thunderous applause.

Uncle Mike stepped forward, his explanation precise and practiced. "These are the Hummingbirds—named for their ability to fly in any direction. They're made from a lightweight, nearly indestructible carbon fiber and diamond composite. A force field protects each, capable of stealth mode, and powered by its pilot's Dragonstone wand."

Mickey continued. "We have completed three ships, with materials for nine more. The plan is to equip each Warbird with two Hummingbirds and expand the launch capabilities at the Complex for training and practice."

"Everyone with a wand will learn to fly them," he added, "except Mandy, who doesn't need one."

Agent Sparks's smile was genuine. "Excellent work. These will reduce our reliance cn individual transporters." Little Mary chimed in with a giggle, "And on carrying people around!"

"Alright," Agent Sparks said, her earlier frustration replaced by enthusiasm, "let's go inside and plan our next move!"

As the applause died, Mandy realized *everything* was about to change. These weren't just another piece of equipment. The Hummingbirds represented something far more critical. Green Hand had always held the tactical advantage—the ability to vanish, strike unexpectedly, inflict pain without warning. Now, for the first time, her team had technology that might match that unpredictability. Stealth mode, energy weapons, the ability to appear and disappear at will—these ships might counter what had made Green Hand seem invincible.

Mandy thought *they're a statement!*

Her uncles and Mickey weren't just creating a new vehicle; the sense that they had always been one step behind was dissolving bit by bit with each precise maneuver of these burgundy ships. Mandy caught Mickey's eye across the courtyard. He was grinning, that familiar cocky smile that said he knew exactly how game-changing this moment was. The Hummingbirds weren't just ships. They were freedom. They were revenge.

As the team's excitement settled, Uncle Tyler's voice cut through the chatter as he leaned against a nearby wall, his posture relaxed but his eyes intense. "I hope, like me, you're hoping we are not alone in this fight. There are magical allies beyond our immediate reach. Some we know, while others we have only heard rumors about."

Mickey, still buzzing from the Hummingbird demonstration, tilted his head. "Like who?"

A knowing smile crossed Uncle Tyler's face. "Mickey! You know ... dragons, for one. Our friends and the ancient guardians of magical balance. Take Thena, for instance—that golden dragon has watched our battles for years. Legend has it she only appears when the magical stakes are truly apocalyptic."

Aunt Laina raised an eyebrow. "And how do you know those legends?"

"From Matty," Uncle Tyler pointed to the family's youngest member. "He visits Owya regularly and talks with the magical ancestors. They've told him that Thena is more than just a dragon. She's a protector of magical lineages who keeps the cosmic balance. But here's the thing—she doesn't just show up. Because not every battle requires her intervention. She watches and waits. And when the moment is absolutely critical as she alone sees it, she acts. They say that when she appears, it means something fundamental is at risk."

A hushed silence fell over the room. For a moment, the triumph of the Hummingbirds felt smaller, overshadowed by the hint of greater magical forces stirring just beyond their understanding.

CHAPTER 6

THE SHAMAN

THE FDM MEETING DRAGGED on, a marathon of strategy and speculation. Mandy's attention fractured between moments of genuine insight and waves of mounting dread; she could taste the tension—metallic, like old pennies on her tongue. Security discussions about the Complex and Warbirds felt almost routine, but her muscles wound tight with anxiety when the conversation turned to locating Green Hand.

Agent Sparks pressed for details. "How did he find you at your grandmother's?" The question hung in the air, sharp as a knife.

Mandy's mind raced as her fingers traced the edge of the conference table, feeling every microscopic imperfection. "Lu

Long and Green Hand were allies. They might have connected their Lizardstones to track each other. Frank Lange was probably involved at one point, but he became greedy and ventured out on his own, creating this island retreat to hide from them." The words tasted like ash in her mouth.

Mandy's nerves frayed as the team crystallized their plan, using her as bait. She thought *Green Hand isn't just another magical threat—he was a force beyond comprehension. Compared to other Lizardstone users, his power dwarfed them all. Loganna's magic in Storyworld, Frank Lange's weak abilities, Lu Long's comparatively passive approach—none matched the raw, terrifying energy of Green Hand. His force fields were impenetrable. His energy bolts could slice through reality itself. He was a predator, and she was the prey!*

When the pain of remembering became unbearable, Mandy created a portal and escaped to *Shadowseeker*, orbiting Earth. She thought, *I doubt Green Hand can sense me out here, but why take any chances?* So, she portalled again to *LUNAR 1*.

The base bustled with unexpected activity. Ducking behind storage boxes, Mandy conjured a disguise spell, transforming into a technician. Clutching a small box, she padded through corridors until she found an empty room. Alone, she let her composure crumble.

Mandy thought, *What am I going to do? What if he penetrates my force field? FDM and Homeland Security seem ready to sacrifice me as bait. Well, not today.* One thought crystallized: *destroy the Lizardstones? No. Without them, no one could stop him. She needed a different approach: find the other two Lizardstones.*

Mandy paced the empty *LUNAR 1* room, her footsteps echoing off the metal walls. Part of her knew this was a crazy idea. Going off alone, without backup, without a plan? Mom would be furious. And the team... they were counting on her. But another part of her, the part that still trembled at the memory of Green Hand's power, whispered that this was her only chance. If she faced him again now, with only two Lizardstones...

She shuddered, hugging her arms around herself. The FDM's plan ran through her mind again - using her as bait, dangling her in front of Green Hand like a worm on a hook. Did they even care what happened to her? Or was she just a pawn, a tool to be sacrificed in this magical arms race? Mandy's fists clenched at her sides. *No.* She refused to be a victim again, waiting helplessly for Green Hand to strike. She would find the stones first, whatever it took. And then, when she faced him again, she would be the one in control.

Mandy returned to the Complex island, bypassing the main buildings. She found her giant lizard herd sleeping around the Red Araza bush and nestled beside Zilla, the largest of them all, a living mountain of scales, wisdom, and ancient magic. Not just a giant creature, but her partner. Her protector.

Zilla's deep red forked tongue darted playfully near her face when she awoke.

"My Queen, why you to nest be?" The giant lizard, six feet tall at the shoulder, had a proud but deferential voice that telepathically buzzed in her skull. Mandy said, "I need your help. Can you locate Lizardstones?"

The giant lizard's large, green eyes reflected something beyond animal intelligence—a primal connection that transcended mere language. Her response rattled in Mandy's ear: "Queen, I do, close, smell Lizardstones with tongue. One, two hundred miles be."

It took Mandy a moment to "interpret" the lizard's language. She remembered how the lizards and the dragons had been trying to adapt their languages to English and how one of the curious artifacts of that translation was the use of short sentences and the use of the English word "be" to indicate many things such as "Yes", "Here", and as a sign of state or status.

As she and Zilla talked, a plan formed, and it was elegant in its simplicity. Frank's ring in Europe. Lu Long from Macau. Green Hand from Africa. That left vast territories unexplored: North America, South America, and Australia.

"South America," Mandy decided. "We start where the oldest magic sleeps." She turned to Zilla. "Hold yourself in readiness, Zilla. Tonight, we will travel the world in search of Lizardstones!"

Mandy thanked Zilla and took the long walk back to the Complex from Zilla's end of the island. She didn't want anyone else in danger, so she kept her plans to herself. She would wait until after everyone went to sleep, then get Zilla and fly around the entire planet if that's what it took to sniff out the Lizardstones. As she approached the Complex buildings, she transported herself directly into her bedroom, hoping to avoid running into anyone. Unfortunately, her mom was waiting there. Her mom spoke angrily, "Where on earth have you been?"

I haven't been on Earth, Mandy thought, but decided not to sass back. "I needed to be alone," she said simply. Her mom sighed and said softly, "Honey, it's dangerous for you to be alone right now."

"I know, Mom," Mandy said. "But everyone is ready to throw me to the wolves to find Green Hand. And I...I...I'm scared." And then, in a whisper with tears running down her face, she said in a barely audible voice, "He hurt me ... badly." Her mom got up from her chair and walked to Mandy. "Oh, honey..."

Mandy moved away, wiping tears from her cheeks. She defiantly declared, "It's not fair. I don't have to go along with this plan if I don't want to." And then she stormed into her bathroom and locked the door behind her.

Her mother sat still for a couple of moments, thinking. Then she went to the bathroom door and spoke, "Honey, everyone, and I mean everyone, knows that. That is why the group's plans ensure your safety first. And why a priority for the boys is to finish making more Hummingbirds so all of us with wands can learn to fly them. Once the plan gets fully complete, *we* will be your protection — in stealth mode. Green Hand won't be able to see us, and we can combine all our firepower to defeat him."

Mandy grumbled through the door, "Yeah. Right. Sounds like a peach of a plan, Mom. Until he kills me to get my Lizardstones. I'm sorry, Mom. No sale." She grabbed her backpack from the hook on the back of the bathroom door and teleported to the CCC cafeteria kitchen. She provisioned herself quickly—water, Lunchables, fruit, and a few energy bars. A GPS device from the lockers completed her kit. Then she hurried out the door and across the polished floor to the array of M-Force lockers, opened hers, removed her poncho, and put it on. Glancing around, she cloaked herself and teleported out of the Complex and back to the giant lizard nest. *I'm sure Mom has figured out that I've left the Complex by now*, she thought. *No need to wait until dark.*

"Zilla," she called, "we leave now." The giant lizard approached with a powerful grace that never failed to remind Mandy of just how formidable these creatures were. With a practiced gesture, she held out her left hand and summoned a Red Araza fruit from the nearby bush. Using magic now felt as natural as breathing. The fruit floated into her backpack, which she slung over her shoulder.

A protective, streamlined energy field shimmered around her and Zilla—not just a shield, but a statement of her growing magical prowess. The field allowed them to shoot into the air, leaving the island behind like a memory. "South America, here we come," she told the lizard, her voice carrying a mix of hope and desperation. "Zilla, start sniffing for Lizardstones!"

The GPS device emerged from her backpack, its screen displaying a map of South America like a battlefield strategy. Mandy plotted a meticulous course down the Atlantic coast, creating a search corridor one hundred miles wide. Her cloaking spell wrapped around them like a second skin, rendering them invisible to ground observers and radar alike. They maintained a steady altitude of 500 feet, close enough to search but far enough to remain undetected. Hours blurred together as they crisscrossed the continent. Mandy's legs ached from gripping Zilla's scales, her muscles screaming with each subtle shift and turn. The wind whipped at her face, bringing tears to her eyes even as she squinted against the sun's harsh glare. The scents in the air were many—tropical plants, dense forests, the flat, oil-soaked smell of cities, and the sweet scent of wide, raging rivers. The landscape below transformed from coastal plains to thick jungle, a green tapestry of potential hiding places. Midnight approached, and exhaustion whispered its siren song of surrender.

"We need to rest," Mandy said, and she selected a secluded clearing in the jungle. Zilla nodded, and Mandy took them quickly down to a soft landing. Once on the ground, Zilla's oversized leg became a stepping platform, helping her descend wearily. They created a makeshift camp. Zilla pulled leafy branches from trees in huge mouthfuls that became their bed, carefully arranged to provide at least minimal comfort. Zilla curled protectively around Mandy, her cooling body starkly contrasting to the jungle's humid warmth. She appreciated the giant living shield, a reminder that she wasn't alone in this dangerous hunt.

Mandy willed a lightweight force field to materialize around them with a soft snap, its surface mimicking the surrounding terrain. Invisible. Safe. For now. Dinner was practical—water conjured from thin air, apricot-flavored energy bars that tasted like compressed determination. The GPS revealed their progress: a meager tenth of the continent covered. The sigh that escaped Mandy carried the weight of mounting frustration. Her hand found Zilla's thickly scaled side—a contact that was part comfort, part connection. Sleep came quickly, born of exhaustion and the knowledge that tomorrow would bring another long day of searching.

Four more days passed. Dawn to dusk, an endless cycle of hope and acceptance. Her earbuds periodically connected her to the Complex, a steady stream of urgent calls she consistently ignored. They didn't understand. The threat was real. Too real.

The Peruvian Andes rose beneath them as the fifth day's evening light painted the sky a deep purple and orange. Zilla's mental voice cut through her weary contemplation: "My Queen! I sense be. Lizardstone; that direction."

Mandy's energy ball engaged instantly. A village approached, nestled almost invisibly among the mountain shadows. "My Queen, smell two stones be close!" Not one stone. Two. Mandy knew exactly what that meant, and the implication struck her like a wall of ice: Green Hand was here!

On landing, Mandy ordered the giant lizard to conceal herself in the forest shadows of the surrounding jungle. *"I'll call for you if I need you,"* she said to Zilla in her mind. The lizard bowed obediently and, with astonishing speed and stealth, disappeared into the trees.

Mandy's cloaking force field shimmered like heat waves as she floated silently toward the village. Darkness cloaked the settlement, broken only by the solitary sight and smell of a sentry's small fire—a lonely spark against the night's ink-black canvas.

Her heart pounded against her ribs as she drifted closer, so loud she feared they might hear it even over the crackling of the sentry's fire. Sweat beaded on her forehead despite the night's chill, and she wiped her palms on her jeans, trying to still their trembling. Mandy moved smoothly and deliberately, controlling each breath. A cluster of small huts seemed to breathe with an ancient stillness. Turning a corner, she saw an eerie green light seeping from a large hut, set apart like a malevolent beacon. Isolated. Protected by the mountainside's massive shadow.

Paranoia prickled along her spine. She scanned the surroundings, every sense hyper-alert, before drifting toward the hut's adobe wall. The dark tan surface seemed to absorb her cloaked form, rough and uneven beneath her magical passage. A small window beckoned—an unexpected vulnerability in the hut's defenses. Voices drifted through. Sharp. Dangerous.

Green Hand's voice sliced through the silence. "So, Shaman, you still refuse to join me?"

The Shaman—small in stature, proud and defiant, wearing a headdress with feathers of impossibly varied colors and a Lizardstone centered like a third eye—faced Green Hand, a green aura dancing around the shaman's head like an ethereal crown. "This is no place for you. You are an evil man. Leave me and my people in peace." The Shaman was an elder, his weathered face etched with deep lines that spoke of a long life in the high mountains. A piercing intensity shone from his dark eyes, and a coiled grace, belying his age, imbued his movements.

As Mandy watched, transfixed, a deadly dance unfolded. Green Hand circled the table, the Shaman mirroring his movements with unexpected grace. Her eyes locked onto the source of the green aura—the headdress! Her breath caught. The fourth Lizardstone! Trapped behind her cloaking spell, she could only watch.

The Shaman's eyes rose to look at Green Hand. He shook his head pityingly. "I knew your father. He was a gentle man, a kind man. A benevolent leader who used magic for the benefit of his people, not for his own gain."

"That's why I killed him to get this," Green Hand snarled. A green, sizzling energy bolt erupted from his hand. The bolt passed through the Shaman like he was smoke, then began to move—not randomly, but with calculated, terrifying intelligence — carving a precise circle beneath the ceiling. Somehow, Mandy could sense that the bolt was ... waiting. Then, the bolt struck with impossible speed. No time for a scream. Just a flash of green mist, and then—nothing. The Shaman was gone, and his headdress lay on the dusty tile floor before Green Hand.

He lifted it slowly, savoring its feel, and placed it on his head. The moment the headdress touched Green Hand's skin, the Lizardstone flared with blinding light. Mandy watched, transfixed, as the stone seemed to liquefy, flowing like molten metal across Green Hand's forehead. His skin absorbed it hungrily, the green glow spreading through his veins until his entire body pulsed with the eerie light. He threw back his head and laughed, the sound echoing with newfound power. As Mandy watched, his muscles bulged and grew. The surrounding air shimmered with heat, and the ground seemed to tremble at his feet. When he looked up again, his eyes blazed with a horrifying green. Mandy thought he looked as if he had lost all his humanity. His words erupted in a roar that shook the earth itself, a shockwave of pure magical energy: "No one can stop me now!"

Mandy felt the force of it like a physical blow, driving the air from her lungs. This was beyond anything she had ever witnessed. The power of two Lizardstones united in one being, fueled by rage and hatred, defied comprehension. In that moment of transformation, Mandy understood something fundamental: this was more than a hunt for stones. This was a war for magical sovereignty—and she had to be the victor.

Survival instinct exploded through Mandy's body. Somehow, Mandy knew that if she wanted to live beyond this moment, she needed to leave instantly! As she flew as fast as she could into the jungle, her mind called Zilla, commanding her to be ready for her. She swooped down toward where she'd left her, then wrapped her energy ball around the massive creature and shot straight up into the sky as high as she could!

Every muscle in Mandy's body burned as she pushed herself faster, higher, pouring every ounce of strength into propelling them upward. The edges of her vision blurred and darkened, exhaustion threatening to drag her down into unconsciousness. But she gritted her teeth and held on, refusing to succumb. Not now. Not when their very survival hinged on this desperate, impossible escape. Mandy feared that since he now possessed two stones, Green Hand might be able to sense her presence. She closed her eyes, focused her mind, and she and Zilla disappeared from the sky as they teleported into *Shadowseeker*. Present for a fraction of a microsecond and cloaked, she then teleported them both to *LUNAR 1*.

Remaining cloaked yet again, she and Zilla hurried into and through the greenhouse. Eight acres of protective trees, plants, bushes, and greenery swallowed them, providing layer upon layer of concealment. Only then, surrounded by silent plants and a controlled atmosphere, did Mandy allow herself to breathe.

At that moment, Mandy realized the truth: the hunt had become something entirely different. A *reckoning* was coming.

CHAPTER 7

SETTING THE TRAP

A LOW GROWL IN HER mind woke Mandy up. It took her a few minutes to remember where she was. Sighing, she thought, *Gracias a Dios, we made it!*

Zilla stood beside her, massive and tense, her body coiled like a spring ready to unleash. NASA technicians moved through *LUNAR 1's* greenhouse, oblivious to the magical fugitive in their midst.

"It's okay," Mandy whispered mentally to Zilla. *"They won't see us."* She pulled her hood low, dropping the force field around herself but keeping it around the giant lizard. *"Stay here,"* she commanded. *"I'll be back."*

Although her massive face seemed to reject the idea, the enormous lizard's eyes narrowed, and she responded in Mandy's head, "Be yes, my Queen."

Mandy's sudden appearance in the greenhouse startled the technicians. One of them even dropped the boxes of seedlings she was carrying. "Sorry!" Mandy said as she helped pick up the box. "Let me help you."

A NASA manager she recognized approached. He raised his clipboard. "Oz," he said, surprised, "you weren't scheduled—"

"Uh...I wanted to double-check the Oxy-ginators," Mandy replied. "I guess I didn't ask if that was OK." Before he could respond, she was gone, her destination firmly in mind.

The Communications Center.

Mandy hurried inside. Seeing a technician who had the duty staffing the Communications Center, she politely asked him for his forgiveness, explaining that she needed to have a classified communication. Once the man left the Center, she adjusted the receiver's communication frequency to that of the classified FDM channel and listened for a few minutes. Since there was no ongoing radio chatter, she took a breath and said into the microphone, "Complex, this is Oz. Come in."

"Oz, we read you," a metallic-sounding voice said somewhat guardedly. "Ma'am, I have to ask what you are doing on this frequency, and why aren't you using your standard comms?" Mandy pushed back. "I'll explain later. Please gather everyone in the CCC briefing area now. Once everyone is there, patch me in. This is priority Zulu. Repeat, priority Zulu. I'll re-connect in ten minutes. Oz, out." Mandy switched off the radio and closed her eyes to think.

Was it a dream? Did I see Green Hand kill that little man he called Shaman? Yes! It __was__ real! And now Green Hand has two Lizardstones, making him even more powerful. And my friends and family! I can't risk the possibility that he can track me down! So, I can't go back to the Complex and endanger everyone else, especially Grandma and the others who cannot protect themselves from his deadly magic.

Mandy broke her train of thought, walked to the water dispenser, and drank three cups of water. She sank into a brown leather chair, pondering her next move. Finally, she looked at a large digital clock on the wall to her left. Its glowing blue numbers told her she had to reconnect to the Complex in one minute. She sighed deeply and made up her mind: Agent Sparks was right! They had to take the fight to Green Hand on *their* terms — not his.

Mandy got up and returned to the communications console. Once powered up, she spoke into the microphone, "This is Oz. Is everyone there?"

"Mand...Oz, this is Cash. Are you alright?"

Mandy smiled. "Yeah. I'm fine. But I need to explain what's happened. It's ... incredible!"

Over the next half hour, Mandy explained how she had searched for the remaining Lizardstones and what had happened last night in Peru. As strong as she tried to be, she could hear the fear in her voice as she explained how Green Hand had killed the Shaman — and that he now wielded two Lizardstones.

After a momentary silence, Mandy added, "Team, Agent Sparks was right. We need to follow through on the plan. We need to set the trap for Green Hand before he fully assimilates his new strength. And I don't think we have much time."

"Oz, this is Gail," Agent Sparks's voice sounded cold, professional, and focused. "Come to the CCC, and we'll work out the last details."

Mandy insisted, "No. I can't risk that. I'm afraid he might sense me anywhere now, even through my force field. We need to decide where to call him, and I'll meet you there."

"But where are you?" asked Agent Sparks. "Can't say, for the same reasons. But I'm safe," Mandy replied. Her hazel eyes narrowed. "Where should we stage our attack?"

Agent Wylee Conners folded his arms, his voice low and deliberate. "If I were him, I'd stay where I'm strongest. We need to catch him off guard. Take it to the Sahara—his comfort zone becomes our advantage. Vast, remote, and with no civilians to worry about. It's the best shot we've got."

After an intense discussion, they decided the Sahara Desert was the right place to go. Each member of the M-Force would fly a cloaked Hummingbird to the Sahara by first going through the portal to *Warbird 1,* which was still patrolling the Mediterranean Sea.

From *Warbird's* location, the Hummingbirds could quickly fly into position in the Sahara. Once there, they could signal Oz on their coordinates so she could transport there and make herself detectable to Green Hand.

Mandy was on board with all that. But she also suggested that the youngest members of the M-Force stay at the Complex to provide magical protection for Grandma and the non-magical parents. Plus, she reasoned, they couldn't fly a Hummingbird since they didn't wield a wand. Although Jenny and Joey protested, the others convinced them that protection duty was an important job as well.

Agent Conners stepped forward, his voice firm and commanding. "Listen up. This wizard is no fool, and he has the firepower to back it up. We need to execute this plan cleanly, with no mistakes. Timing will be everything." He traced a map of the Sahara on the holo-display. "We'll have no second chances if Green Hand senses us coming. Everyone needs to know their role cold before we move out."

"We'll need to account for his environmental advantage," J.T. said, tapping a finger on the desert map. "The heat and sand could interfere with our technology and spells if we're not careful. I suggest we prep cooling spells and visibility enhancers—there's no point going in blind just because the sun's playing favorites."

Conners nodded in agreement and surveyed the room, his gaze cutting through it like a laser. "I don't care how good you think you are—this guy has two stones, which changes the game. Keep your heads and stick to your roles; if anyone has cold feet, now's the time to speak up." His eyes scoured the room, daring anyone to question him. He said, "No second chances on this one, people."

The following day, after receiving word that the Hummingbirds were circling a section of the Sahara Desert, Mandy teleported to *Shadowseeker* from *LUNAR 1* with Zilla. She then teleported to the designated coordinates in the Sahara.

Mandy cloaked Zilla in a force field with her wand and transported the giant lizard to the location where she had first fought Green Hand. Then Mandy used her Lizardstone to create a green portal and portalled back to where she left Zilla. By using her amulet, Mandy hoped it would alert Green Hand of her presence. Next, Mandy used her Lizardstone ring to create a protective green force field around herself, hoping it would deflect Green Hand's energy bolts more effectively than her blue one had before.

Mandy's hazel eyes narrowed, her breath catching in her throat. The memory of the Shaman's death burned behind her eyelids—a brutal reminder of Green Hand's escalating power. Two Lizardstones, same as her, but with so much more power. The thought made her stomach churn. This isn't just about me anymore, she realized. It's about everyone I love. Her mind flickered to Grandma, her parents, Jenny and Joey, and all the others who couldn't defend themselves against this magical threat.

The weight of responsibility pressed against her chest, a tangible thing that made each breath a conscious effort. Fear clawed at the edges of her resolve. Green Hand had killed the Shaman with such casual brutality. What would he do to her family? No. She wouldn't let that happen. Mandy's fists clenched, green energy sparking between her fingers. She hardened her resolve like tempered steel — she might be scared, but she was finished with fear.

"Kijani M'kono!" she called into the empty Sahara, her voice carrying a mix of defiance and resolve. "I am here to face you. And this time, I'm not running. Once I beat you, I will take your Lizardstones and do with them what I will!" She shot a green energy ball high into the sky and then repeated that three times until an eerie feeling came over her. She knew … the battle was engaged!

An instant later, Mandy saw green energy balls flying toward her from the sky. This group bounced harmlessly off her force field. Then she sensed another barrage of energy balls heading toward her and raised her left hand, drawing each sizzling ball into the palm of her hand. She looked at the glowing, sizzling energy balls. Then, she leveled her hand in the direction from which they had come, gathered a massive volume of wind into her lungs, and blew a tremendous blast of wind onto her palm. An incredibly long and dense bolt of green energy flew back toward the source of the onslaught.

The bolt didn't get far. Fifty yards from Mandy, it exploded in mid-air, revealing a large floating platform that had been cloaked by magic. Standing near the front edge of the floating platform was ... Green Hand! At least one hundred warriors armed with energy spears surrounded him on three sides. Mandy's battle-experienced eyes recognized them as identical to those she had encountered before. She could also see both of Green Hand's Lizardstones. They glowed with the raw fuel of his evil emotions. Gathering her thoughts, she dreaded the battle about to begin.

With all her might, she raised both hands and shot a steady stream of energy from her Dragonstone and Lizardstones. Green Hand, levitating in mid-air, deflected most of her attack, but not all of it. Some of her power struck a few warriors, instantly vaporizing them. Green Hand returned fire with his Lizardstones. He commanded his men to "Fire at will!" and Mandy strained mightily to repel the energy bolts sent her way. In that instant, a rainbow of colored energy bolts rained down from the sky on Green Hand and his army. The Hummingbirds had engaged in the battle as planned!

Below, Zilla ate the fruit of the Red Araza bush Mandy had left with her. The giant lizard grew to three times her usual size in seconds, standing over 15 feet tall at its shoulder. Fueled by the power of the fruit, Zilla belched four consecutive green energy balls, striking and destroying the floating platform from which the enemy was fighting and causing Green Hand's army to fall to the desert sands far below. With the warriors scattered, the Hummingbirds darted through the sky, picking them off one by one. As the number of Green Hand's warriors diminished, the Hummingbirds also took shots at him. Protected by his force field and continuing to fire directly at Mandy, Green Hand also tried to shoot back at the Hummingbirds — but they were just too fast!

Mandy sensed that Green Hand was up to something, but she couldn't quite make out what it was. Suddenly, a pulse of bright green light from Green Hand's headdress filled the sky, eliminating the Hummingbird's cloaking spell. Mandy shouted over her comms, "He somehow disabled your cloaking spells. They can see you now. Take evasive maneuvers!"

She doubled her rate of fire toward Green Hand but couldn't penetrate his force field. Just then, another pulse of green light of a different shading burst from Green Hand's headdress. Agent Spark's voice rang out over the comms, "Red Alert! That last blast of light from his headdress gave us a tremendous problem! Someone just launched every missile in the Middle East! Even missiles from U.S. ships have fired without authorization!"

Uncle Tyler responded, "Hummingbirds will shoot them down as soon as they reach us!" Agent Spark reacted immediately. "Negative, repeat, negative! The hummingbirds aren't targeting you! The trajectories appear to be directed at every major city along the shore of the Mediterranean!"

Mandy broke in, "It's him. He's forced a diversion that the Hummingbirds can't ignore! You must intercept and stop the missiles from reaching their targets." Mandy's mother's voice was icy, calm, and urgent. "No, Mandy. We cannot leave you to fight him alone!"

"You have to, Mom!" Mandy replied. "You can't let all of those innocent people die! J.T. and Gemini get to the *Warbird* and help. Prism and Atlas stay at the Complex as backup."

Each of the Hummingbirds sped off, getting coordinates to a targeted city from the Complex. Mandy looked at Green Hand.

A devilish grin was spreading across his face. She braced herself using her wand and strengthened her force field. Then, she began firing at Green Hand again. At the same time, another fusillade of Zilla's giant energy balls decimated Green Hand's army.

Green Hand focused his attention on the giant lizard. He narrowed his eyes and blasted an energy bolt from his headdress, which rattled the protective sphere around Zilla so hard it knocked her to the ground. But before he could deliver a finishing blow, Mandy summoned a portal and transported Zilla away from the Sahara, firing at Green Hand to draw his attention.

He turned, screaming, "You may have saved her for now, but once I've taken care of all of you, I will become her master, and she will do my bidding!"

Another burst of light from Green Hand's headdress immobilized Mandy's arms and legs just as she was about to teleport away. Energy bolts from the spears of the twenty remaining warriors of Green Hand's army then struck Mandy's force field, delivering seething pain throughout her body.

Mandy felt something she rarely experienced: pure, unfiltered terror. In Storyworld, she had confronted an evil sorceress. She'd rescued the stranded astronauts. She'd transformed entire buildings into titanium. But this? This was different. Her mind raced through every magical trick she knew. The Lizardstone ring pulsed against her skin as if it were trying to tell her something. She coached herself: *Remember what Danny always says*: *Magic isn't just about power. It's about creativity.*

The Hummingbirds darted overhead, their energy bolts creating a rainbow of magical resistance. Mandy knew they were buying her time, but time for what? They couldn't maintain that defense indefinitely. One of Green Hand's energy bolts nearly penetrated her force field. Close. Too close.

A huge torrent of power surged in Mandy's breast. She bellowed, "NO! I DON'T THINK SO! I will not die here! Not today. Not like this." The Lizardstone at her throat warmed, responding to her determination. Somewhere between a scientific calculation and a magical intuition, a plan formed in Mandy's mind. She summoned all her will to secure her force field, then, with her remaining strength, whispered one more spell as Green Hand's onslaught threatened to penetrate and kill her.She put her plan into action. "Stop!" she cried with a painful moan. "Please, stop."

Green Hand raised his hand, and his remaining warriors ceased their fire. Mandy's force field flickered, a pale blue membrane growing increasingly transparent each moment.

Mandy's head hung listlessly from her neck. But deep in her magical core, something ancient stirred. The Lizardstone amulet pulsed with a connection to magical bloodlines that transcended her knowledge. Whispered family stories about unexplained moments of magic and power suddenly felt real, tangible. And in that moment, suspended between survival and destruction, Mandy felt a presence. It wasn't Green Hand. Nor was it her family. It was something that felt as if it had been waiting, observing, calculating. Just then, a shadow eclipsed the harsh sunlight of the Sahara.

Something so large and powerful as to almost be beyond imagination was approaching. A brief, painfully bright flash of pure white light filled the sky. "What the..." Green Hand exclaimed as he shielded himself from being incinerated just as his remaining warriors had been.

Thena, the immense golden dragon, thirty-eight feet tall at her shoulder, spewed flame in all directions as she descended through Green Hand's force field and grabbed Mandy within her talons. Shielding Mandy, the dragon flew toward the sun at an unbelievable rate as Green Hand impotently shot fireballs after her. Turning, Thena streaked out of the Sahara and over the Atlantic Ocean, heading for home in Northern Canada.

Mandy, in a profound wave of gratitude and relief so intense it bordered on reverence, thought *Thank you, Thena!* And in that moment, Mandy's mind snapped into a profound realization: she had not just been 'saved.' Something far more significant than a simple intervention had rescued her — it was protection and connection. Another thought now crystallized in her mind: *We're not alone.*

And then she passed out.

CHAPTER 8

THE FIFTH LIZARDSTONE

MANDY WOKE TO THE sound of chatter in her earbud. She felt dazed. And she could feel a cool wind in her hair. She looked up at the belly of a gigantic golden dragon. Its vast wings curtained the sky. It took a moment to recall that she was being flown to safety by Thena, the golden dragon. Mandy looked down; all she could see were lakes and treetops. She didn't know how long they had been flying, but she guessed they might be over the Canadian forest where Thena and her dragon clan lived.

Mandy felt pain everywhere in her body, and there was a constant ringing in her head. But, as she listened to the communications over her earbud, she smiled to hear that her comrades had successfully intercepted every missile Green Hand had launched. Then she heard, "Oz, this is Command. Come in."

Taking a deep breath and gathering her thoughts, she responded, "This is Oz; go ahead."

"Good to hear your voice, Oz. We were anxious." Mandy recognized Agent Sparks' voice and said, "I had some help. I barely got away. This is far from over. I think I should go silent for a while to avoid detection. I'll check back in four hours."

A few minutes later, Mandy felt Thena descend. She watched as the dragon flew straight toward a group of trees and closed her eyes, expecting to crash into them! Mandy thought, *This dragon is too big, and we'll never make it!* But they passed harmlessly through a thin layer of branches and entered a massive cave in the side of a mountain. Thena slowed and landed on her two hind legs, gently flapping her enormous wings to keep her front legs above the ground, and then slowly lowered Mandy to the cave floor.

"Can be walked, Mandy the Witch?" Thena asked. "I... think so," Mandy replied with some effort. She used Thena's leg for support and stood up, taking a few tentative steps before coming to a stop. "Yes, I can walk. But just barely."

"Maybe you ride be," the dragon said. She lowered her massive shoulder low enough for Mandy to crawl onto the dragon's broad back. Thena rose again and — with surprising grace — walked toward what appeared to be a solid rock wall some fifty yards away. The dragon's weight, even at this pace, caused the ground to tremble, but her gait never slackened as she simply passed right through the wall! Mandy thought, *A force field. I wonder how that got conjured up?*

Her eyes grew wide with excitement and disbelief as Thena stopped at the edge of a high, rocky ledge. Before them lay a tremendous cave of such a size that Mandy gasped! She could not see the far side of the chamber because it was so distant. Scores of dragons — *some even bigger than Thena* — flew overhead and across the vast expanse. More were sitting and lounging on distant cliffs and on the cave floor several hundred feet below. A soft light, reminiscent of sunlight diffused through a light cloud cover, illuminated the enormous space.

Mandy asked, "Thena, how did you find this place?"

The dragon smiled before answering. "Sanctuary, made by Josef Phefvenscen. Be he Phef Wizard's eldest son. When Phef left Earth, be he took the oldest dragons with him. Phef told Josef to be protect youngest dragons. Josef took Paction's granddaughter and one-fifty dragons. They travelled here, Queen. Then created this place. Hide dragons from evils. Protect bloodline, be."

Pain suddenly overcame Mandy. She closed her eyes and moaned loudly. Thena moved her noble head and examined Mandy closely. She said, "Mandy, you be need help now." Gathering Mandy in one of her massive, clawed paws, the enormous dragon lept off the ledge and glided swiftly down to the cave floor.

Mandy woke on a soft green bed of moss and grass. She felt very weak.

She tried to focus on her watch and thought, *"Oh no — I was supposed to contact the Complex hours ago!"* She tried her earbud comms, but no one responded. Looking around, Mandy noticed a small orange dragon, only ten feet tall at the shoulder, sitting beside her. The dragon bowed its head and said, "Device won't be here, Mandy Witch."

Mandy struggled to sit up. "I have to communicate with my family..." But the pain overwhelmed her, and she slumped back down onto the mossy bed. "Return soon be, Thena," the dragon said. Mandy could feel her strength ebbing away. She thought, *I must have internal injuries*, and *if I don't get help quickly...*

And with that thought, she passed out again.

This time, Mandy awoke with the sensation of water on her face. She looked up and saw the orange dragon with a cluster of leaves in its mouth. Water slowly dripped from the leaves and onto Mandy's forehead. Weakly, Mandy grabbed some of the moss around her and used it like a sponge to wipe her face. She smiled at the dragon.

Feeling a large vibration through the ground, Mandy looked around slowly and saw Thena walking toward her.

The orange dragon told Mandy, "Mouth open, Witch. Quietly be. Still, and move not!" Mandy did as she was told, but her eyes widened, and her body stiffened involuntarily as Thena moved her gigantic head to within an inch of Mandy's and said, "Mouth open!" As Mandy did so, the golden dragon, with surprising delicacy, squirted something directly into Mandy's mouth. Mandy's mouth clamped shut as Thena nodded and said softly, "Swallow, Witch." Mandy could not help but close her eyes and do as she had been told.

In an instant, she felt better. It was like she could feel her wounds healing and her body growing stronger. She felt great! Sitting upright, Mandy said, "Was that unicorn saliva?" Thena nodded. "Be, Mandy Witch. Found a unicorn. She gave saliva."

Mandy said, "Thena, may I leave this place now?" Thena said, "Yourself not be, Mandy Witch. Dragons only through barrier. Be no fear; I will take you out when ready."

Mandy said, "Thena, I am forever indebted to you. But I must go. Thank you for saving me." The great golden dragon shook her huge head and again lowered her shoulder so Mandy could climb onto her back. "Owe nothing, Mandy Witch. Friends. Together be. We fly now."

Seated on Thena's neck, Mandy marveled as the dragon flew high into the air and circled the sanctuary's interior. Then, Thena banked slightly to her right to approach the ledge that led to the opening to the outside world. Mandy's earbuds crackled to life as they passed through the force field. She heard the Complex trying to reach her. "Can we please land, Thena?" Mandy asked. The great golden dragon nodded, slowed down, and positioned itself for a soft landing. Once safely on the ground, Mandy climbed down. She thanked Thena with a fierce hug along the dragon's scaly neck, summoned her wand, and created a blue portal to the Complex.

The moment she materialized, the transport area erupted in chaos. Her mother rushed forward, pulling her into a tight embrace that spoke of hours of worry. They held each other, tears mixing, the relief palpable.

"We don't have much time," Mandy whispered, pulling back. "Green Hand is still out there." Her mom nodded, wiping her eyes. Everyone is in the briefing area. They've been strategizing non-stop."

Mandy wiped her tears from her cheeks and hugged her mom again. She said, "OK. Let's go." And the two of them headed to the CCC briefing area.

The crowd greeted Mandy with cheers and hugs. *It feels so good to be back here,* Mandy thought. *But we must get to work!* Thanking everyone again, Mandy went to the front of the area to address the assembly and said, "Nice job with the missiles, team!"

A round of applause swept the room, and as it receded, everyone started peppering her with questions about what had happened, how she had gotten away, where she had been, and so on. But Mandy just motioned for everyone to quiet down. "Please," she said, "I'll explain later. For now, we need to find the fifth Lizardstone. It's the only way to defeat Green Hand. And if he finds it first…" She left the dire meaning hanging in the air.

Gina leaned forward, her hazel eyes intense. "So, how do we find it before he does?"

Mandy explained, "I tracked down the Shaman's stone by following magical traces. But this feels different. More complicated somehow." A small voice cut through the tension. "It won't work that way."

Everyone turned. Six-year-old Matty sat on his mother's lap, his expression unexpectedly serious. Mickey chuckled. "Seriously? What could you possibly—"

"Mickey," his mother warned, "let the boy speak." She turned Matty so that he could see her face clearly. "Matty, honey, why won't we find the Lizardstone that way?"

Matty looked at his mother with a knowing look for a six-year-old. Then he looked directly at Mandy, his eyes holding an unsettling intensity as he said calmly, "The fifth Lizardstone is in Owya. *In the volcano.*" A beat of complete silence followed. Even the air seemed to hold its breath.

Mandy knelt before him, her voice soft but urgent. "Matty, how do you know this?" The little boy just smiled—a smile that made the adults in the room suddenly feel … very small.

CHAPTER 9

LOGANNA'S SCEPTER

O F COURSE! MANDY THOUGHT. *The fifth Lizardstone is on Loganna's scepter! When we defeated Loganna in Storyworld, Phef the Wizard took Loganna's scepter and transported Loganna to the Spirit World after the Parasol was destroyed.*

"Yes! I have to go to Owya!" Mandy said, standing up. "I have to get Loganna's scepter!"

Just then, an alarm sounded. Agent Conners' voice cut through the intercom like a whip, sharp and precise. "Red Alert! This is no drill. The Complex is under active assault!"

Everyone rushed to the CCC to see what was happening. The giant main screen showed the view from one of the security cameras atop the building. High above, Green Hand was hovering on a platform, armed with weapons, firing green energy bolts at the force field protecting the Complex.

Instantly, Mandy took charge.

"J.T., get into the courtyard and do whatever you can to strengthen my force field. Jenny, we need Prism! Mary..." and a flash of orange flame interrupted her as Mary and Jane joined hands to form Gemini.

"You need Gemini!" both heads of the two-headed flying tiger roared.

Mandy smiled. "Absolutely. Next, M-Force, man your Hummingbirds." She turned to her dad. "Dad, you need to lead everyone else to *LUNAR 1*. You know the way. They'll need help navigating through *Shadowseeker* to reach the *Lunar 1* portal. Take Grandma, Mrs. Sparks, and the rest of the family. Matty, too."

Her dad nodded quickly. Concern rimmed his eyes.

Agent Sparks asked, "What can we do?" Mandy paused and then shook her head. "Go with Dad. You can't fight Green Hand's magic."

Agent Sparks started to argue but then simply nodded and turned to her team, ordering them to gear up and follow Mandy's dad through the portal Mandy had just conjured. She said, "Dad, this will connect you to *Shadowseeker*. Hurry, there's little time."

Mandy watched as husbands and wives gave each other brief, intense hugs. Then, fathers and mothers hurriedly hugged their children. Mandy looked at Grandma, smiled, and nodded as her dad escorted the older woman to the portal. Once the magical M-Force was alone, they silently summoned their wands from their Dragonstones and joined hands like a team preparing to start a game.

Uncle Tyler said, "I love all of you and am proud to be part of this family. This is up to us now!"

Mandy said, "OK, everyone, listen up quickly. I need to go to the Spirit World and bring Loganna's scepter back. Fight Green Hand as best you can, but.." and she pointed to the portal she'd created a few moments before... "...go through that portal if you think there's a chance he might get by you. I've enchanted the portal to close after the last of you go through it. If you don't escape through it, he'll follow everyone to *LUNAR 1* and kill them all, so don't be a hero! Do you understand?" Everyone nodded their agreement, understanding what was at stake.

Mandy watched as her family rushed out of the CCC like a band of soldiers charging into battle. Despite her desire to fight alongside them, she had to complete her mission. She reached into a pocket on the inside of her poncho and pulled out Gigi's tiger's-eye stone. She then wrapped her right fist around the stone, closed her eyes, and disappeared from the Earth.

Opening her eyes, she found herself ...somewhere ... and surrounded by a dense fog. She thought, *This is where Gigi and I started when we first came to Owya. But Izzy the Brave guided us through this fog to the next section of Owya. I don't know which way to go. How am I supposed to get through this to the volcano?*

Mandy wanted to start walking, but there was no sign of which way to go. She tried to use her magic, but the Lizardstones and Dragonstone did not respond. So she paused, cleared her mind, and looked at the tiger's eye stone in her palm.

Suddenly, a soft voice spoke behind her. "I thought you might need my help."

"Matty!" Mandy exclaimed. "Do you know the way to the volcano?" Matty shook his head. "No, but I know how you can get there."

Puzzled, Mandy looked at him for a long moment. Then, when he said nothing, she asked, "Matty! How?"

"There are barriers to get to the center of Owya," Matty said, his brown eyes glowing. "Follow your heart. Take one step at a time. Calm yourself. Use your mind. Then let your spirit soar."

"What? Matty, that makes no sense!" Mandy said, shaking her head. "Tell me how to get through the barriers."

Mandy was having a hard time focusing on Matty. He appeared to be ... *fading!*

"I have to go, Mandy," Matty replied calmly and serenely. "Hurry and come back to save us." And then he vanished into the surrounding fog.

Just great! Mandy thought. *Matty has the power to come and go into Owya, and he strands me here with an earful of gibberish, leaving me to navigate the five barriers myself.*

"Wait!" she said aloud. "There are five barriers! Matty *was* giving me instructions! He said five things!" She tried to recall his exact words. "He first said, 'Follow your heart.' ... I wonder?"

Mandy looked at the tiger's eye stone in her hand and held it over her chest, above her heart. Nothing happened. She slowly turned in a circle, hoping something would show her the way. Suddenly, a bright yellow beam of light shot straight ahead from the stone, and she came to a halt. *Follow my heart*, she thought, as she walked toward the beam.

After what seemed like hours of walking, the fog lifted, and the next barrier of the fire land appeared before her. *The fire!* She thought. *I have to cross the fire. What was the next thing Matty said?* she asked herself. *Calm yourself? No! Take one step at a time!*

She nodded. *I need to walk through this one step at a time.* And so she did, carefully placing one foot directly in front of the other. Mandy remembered how she and Gigi crossed the flaming land, following directly behind her ancestor, Felix Cooper, as he led them across.

The heat wasn't just external. It crawled inside her skin, testing her resolve. Each step felt like walking through liquid memory—her ancestors' footsteps burning beneath her feet. The flames whispered ancient challenges, daring her to prove her worth.

Crossing this barrier seemed to take longer than the previous one, and Mandy worried about her family fighting Green Hand. But then she remembered that time in Owya differs from time on Earth. Mandy recalled that when she was here with Gigi, what she thought would take hours only took a few minutes on Earth.

After a while, Mandy approached the shore of the next barrier: the endless lake. But instead of the calm lake she and Gigi crossed on a raft guided by Charles the Grey, the lake raged with stormy waves. Mandy remembered Matty's next instruction: 'Calm yourself' — and guessed the storm reflected — her emotions! *But how do I calm myself with all that is happening? Mom! Mom always says to close my eyes and take three deep breaths when I get upset.*

Mandy moved to the edge of the stormy lake's shore and closed her eyes. She held her right hand out in front of her and opened her palm, letting the tiger's eye stone rest on it. Then she took three deep breaths and stood completely still. The storm wasn't just water and wind. It was emotion made manifest—her fear, her worry for her family, her uncertainty about the mission. Each wave represented a doubt, each gust a moment of potential failure.

When she opened her eyes, the lake was behind her! Somehow, she had crossed it!

Before her now was the dark forest that Charles the Grey and his pack of wolves had guided her and Gigi through. As she approached the forest's shadows, she heard snarling and growls that caused her to back up in fear. *Charlie's wolves protected them from these beasts, whatever they were. How am I going to get through the forest?*

'*Use your mind*' was Matty's instruction. *Great,* Mandy thought, *what does that even mean?*

She closed her eyes as she heard the deep, bone-shaking growls in her ears. She opened her mind, and instead of beastly snarling, she heard an impossibly deep, gravelly voice in her head, speaking a distinct language, but one Mandy recognized: "Away! Land is be ours!"

Giant lizards! But these lizards felt different from the ones she'd met before. Her mind told her these were more ancient, primordial. The growls vibrated through her bones, a language older than words. She spoke out with her mind's voice, but this time, she let her vulnerability show. "Oh, great lizard," she projected, feeling the weight of every ancestral connection, "I am not just a visitor. I am part of something larger."

The massive lizard that emerged from the shadows was unlike anything she'd ever seen—and she'd seen many giant lizards! Its scales weren't just a surface but a living tapestry - deep crimson overlapping in intricate patterns that seemed to shift and breathe. Each scale was the size of her hand, edges razor-sharp yet arranged with an almost architectural precision. Steam rose from its massive nostrils, carrying a scent of ancient earth and something metallic—like old magic. When it moved, the forest floor didn't just shake. It transformed. Trees bent, not from force, but from a profound respect. Roots seemed to part, creating a path without the lizard needing to move them. Its eyes were not animal eyes. They were liquid intelligence, amber-gold with flecks of emerald that seemed to hold entire histories within them. Mandy realized she wasn't just being watched. She was being evaluated by something that had seen civilizations rise and fall—many of them. The great lizard's red tongue flickered between its razor-sharp teeth - each tooth as long as her forearm, gleaming like polished obsidian. But there was no threat in its stance.

This was a council, an ancient judgment. At that moment, Mandy understood this was more than a passage through the territory. This was a test. An ancient ritual of recognition that stretched beyond mere physical boundaries. The lizard wasn't just deciding whether to let her pass - it was measuring her essence, her connection to something far older than herself.

As its emerald-flecked eyes locked with hers, Mandy felt a profound connection to this creature and every magical being that had ever navigated these mystical spaces. Her vulnerability wasn't weakness. It was her strength. She spoke out with her mind's voice: "Oh great lizard. I need your help. I am a Lizard Queen in my land, and an evil force is threatening my herd. I must cross your land to reach the volcano on the other side."

"Who you?" the voice sounded in her head. "What be name?"

"I am ..." Mandy paused and thought, *Should I call out her witch name or her real name?* Finally, she said aloud, "I am Mandy the Witch, daughter of Joy, Granddaughter of Jane, Great-granddaughter of Helen, and direct descendant of Mathias Phefvenscen!"

"Mandy the Witch. Yes, so brethren departed your world says be," the voice responded. Then the voice took on a deeper tone, harsher, accusatory, and demanding, making Mandy shiver. "Some in battle you killed! Some you saved, be."

Then, as if in a premonition, Mandy took two steps backward. She didn't know whether to run away or to fight. After a silent standoff, she bowed to the lizard and said, "I no longer fight giant lizards. Giant lizards are part of my pack, my herd, my family."

The great lizard looked at Mandy for two or three long minutes. Finally, the lizard's eyes narrowed to mere slits in its enormous face, and with a long, slow exhale of breath, the lizard's voice again sounded in her head, "It be so. Climb back. Take to volcano, Witch."

Mandy climbed aboard the lizard, and it immediately sprinted into the forest, racing impossibly fast between towering brown trees that resembled redwoods, their canopies of green and blue leaves high above them. As they ran, dozens of other giant lizards joined them, causing a rumbling sound like a herd of gigantic stampeding elephants. In long minutes, they had left the forest's darkness behind, and all the lizards were looking up at the top of the volcano Mandy knew must have been the one called the Abyss.

The lizard Mandy was riding shrugged, and she dismounted. Mentally, she thanked the lizards and told them she must continue her quest. Almost simultaneously, the giant lizards thought, *"Yes, Witch!"* and turned, sprinting back into the forest's shadows at tremendous speed.

Mandy looked up at the sheer rock face of the volcano, knowing she needed to reach the summit. *"Let your spirit soar,"* Mandy thought, recalling Matty's last words of advice.

She walked to what she felt seemed close to where Rocco and his winged lion landed to carry her and Gigi to the top of the mountain. Then she spread her arms wide and leaped into the air, as if diving off a cliff, and felt herself soaring into the sky, higher and higher, towards the top of the mountain. When she landed on the volcano's rim, she smiled, winked, and said, "Thank you, Matty."

Mandy took a deep breath, looked around, and saw only the barren rock of the volcano's rim. Moving carefully, she leaned over the rim and looked down into the fiery inferno of the Abyss, seeing nothing but flames and smoke.

How am I going to find the scepter in the Abyss? She thought.

"It's over here," a voice behind her said. Mandy spun on her heels and looked in shock at the person who had called her. Loganna!

It <u>was</u> Loganna! But she looked … different. Instead of a wicked-looking, green-skinned witch, she looked serene, composed, and beautiful. Her skin was a pretty shade of olive, and her hair was silky, smooth, and a glistening green that hung down to the middle of her back. And her eyes were a luminous, powerful green, too. Mandy thought, *"She looks like an older version of me!"*

Warily, Mandy spoke sternly, "What are you doing here? I thought you were in…"

"…the Abyss?" Loganna interrupted.

"Well…Yes!" Mandy responded, less sternly. Loganna's lips twitched as if considering a tiny grin. "I should have been. But I'm not. Thanks to you."

"Me?" Mandy said, confused. "Yes, you," Loganna said as she approached Mandy. She took Mandy's hands into her own. "When I heard J.T. call you 'Mandy', and then you picked up my scepter…Well, it filled my heart. I couldn't believe it!"

Mandy's mind was reeling as she tried to process all that. Then, from behind her, Mandy heard Phef's voice! "You see, Mandy, she is also your ancestor."

What?! Mandy's mind raced even faster. *How could this be?* As if he read her mind, Phef continued softly, "It is so. Long ago, Loganna and I were married. And then we had a child. Her name was Mandalina. Loganna … called her Mandy."

Mandy saw tears welling in Loganna's eyes.

"But our Mandy died in a … tragic accident for which Loganna blamed … me…" Phef said as tears welled up in his eyes, too.

Loganna interrupted, "My heart turned to stone, so I devoted the rest of my life to evil and dark magic. And in that mind, I could have destroyed you without a backward glance if I really wanted to do so. But when I saw the scepter bond with you when you picked it up, my heart knew. It understood, and so did I, and in that instant, I healed, and the evil left me."

Mandy's voice caught, a tremor of confusion threading through her words. "But how—" She stopped, the mathematics of ancestry spinning dizzily in her mind. "That makes little sense. How am I your ancestor if your Mandy died?"

Loganna looked down to the ground and spoke haltingly, "I had another child … much later … after I left Phef. He had … gone to have another wife, another family, and I… well, let's just say I behaved badly."

After a long pause, Phef said, "It was a difficult time, and eventually, Loganna ... left her second child. But I had been watching Loganna, so I rescued the child and placed him with a nice family who could not have children. The boy grew up loved and never knew of Loganna. Nor of his magical heritage. Ultimately, ..."

Mandy interrupted, "He was my father's ancestor, right? And that's why the Lizardstones could bond with me, but not with Gina! And that's why I could read Loganna's book of spells!"

"Verily so," said Loganna. "And once I realized that so much good was a part of the long-ago love of Phef and me, I couldn't stay hateful. Phef and I agreed — to go to Owya, expecting my fate to hurl me into the Abyss. But my healed heart kept me here with Phef." Her eyes flowed with tears. Then she softly added, "You looked ... just as I imagined my Mandy would have looked. And now, you look very much like me."

Mandy hugged her. After holding the hug for a long time, Mandy's voice was thick with emotion as she said, "My family. Our family is in danger, fighting an evil man who wields two Lizardstones and vows to kill me to get the two I have. He is very powerful. He almost killed me. I need the scepter to defeat him."

Loganna responded immediately, "It is yours to take!" as she pointed over the volcano's rim behind her. Mandy ran to the rim and looked down. Floating above the flames, far below, Mandy could see the unmistakable glimmer of the fifth Lizardstone affixed at the top of Loganna's scepter. She turned and said, "How do I get down there to get it?"

Loganna smiled. "My darling, you don't have to. Just put out your hand ... and call for it."

Mandy blinked, and then her mind saw the entire story. She moved to the edge of the volcano rim, outstretched her left arm, and called the scepter with a powerful yet loving thought: *Come to me!*

The scepter shot upward at tremendous speed, and in just a moment, it was in her open hand, nearly knocking her to the ground. As she twisted her wrist, pointing the scepter into the sky, a bolt of green energy shot from the Lizardstone and swirled around her. Mandy held on with all her might and then watched as her other two Lizardstones burst from the ring and amulet and circled in the air around the scepter.

"What is happening?!?" Mandy shouted as she turned toward Loganna and Phef.

Before they could answer, Mandy's Dragonstone burst from her cuff bracelet and joined the Lizardstones in the swirl around the scepter. Then, Gigi's tiger's eye stone escaped from the secret pocket of Mandy's poncho and joined the orbiting stones. The stones erupted in a kaleidoscope of light—green as lizard scales, blue as deep ocean, yellow as desert sand. The power wasn't just external; it burrowed into her bones, rewrote her internal map, and hummed with an ancient, familiar song of magic that felt more like remembering than learning.

In another instant, everything was calm.

Mandy looked at the scepter and saw that the four other stones were now embedded in the orb at the top of the scepter, which was now ... solid gold. The four stones surrounded the fifth larger Lizardstone, which sat atop the scepter's orb.

Mandy looked at her ancestors with perfect love, and then, giving a slight nod, she closed her eyes and disappeared from Owya.

CHAPTER 10

THE GREAT AND
POWERFUL

WHEN MANDY OPENED HER eyes, she stood exactly where she had been when she used the tiger's eye stone to enter the Spirit World.

She turned and saw that her blue portal to *Shadowseeker* was still open behind her, so she rushed out of the room, heading for the courtyard. Entering an interior hallway, she ran into Aunt Lilah, carrying Danny in her arms and heading for the Transportation room. Both were bleeding, and Danny appeared to be unconscious.

"Mandy, what happened to you?" Aunt Lilah cried and stumbled to her knees, nearly dropping Danny.

Mandy moved to look at herself in a hallway mirror and was amazed to see that she resembled *an Amazon warrior*. She had to be at least six feet tall and was as muscular as a pro wrestler. She shook her head. "No time. What's the situation out there?" Bending slightly, she picked Danny up with one hand as easily as if he were a doll.

"It's turning bad," Aunt Lilah replied. "Green Hand broke through the force field, and everyone began firing. He brought down an entire wall of the complex onto Laina and me. I blocked most of it and was trying to dig Laina out when he shot down Danny's Hummingbird. Danny crashed into some bushes next to me, so I helped him to the portal." Her voice grew more urgent. "I need to go back and help Laina and…"

Mandy interrupted. "I'll get Aunt Laina. You're injured and need to see Dr. Kate." Waving her scepter in a circle, Danny and Aunt Lilah disappeared in a flash as she transported them directly through the portal. Without another moment's hesitation, Mandy ran to the courtyard and found Mickey trying to free his mother from the debris of the fallen wall. Looking around, she saw Green Hand battling all of her giant lizards and J.T.! With a slight wave of her scepter, Mandy threw the entire mass of the fallen wall's stone and steel directly at Green Hand! As he blocked the onslaught with a green energy field, Mandy sent Mickey and Aunt Laina through the portal with another wave of her scepter.

She then yelled with such a powerful voice that everyone ceased fire and turned to look at her. "Stop! I am here now. Fight me and me alone! If you dare!"

Green Hand let out a mighty laugh, and Mandy watched as he encircled J.T. and the lizards with a force field, then closed his fists to shrink the field in an attempt to crush them all. He yelled across the battleground, "Ha! I've been waiting for you to show your face. So that you can watch these weaklings die!"

Mandy pointed her scepter at him and fired a wide beam of blue energy. It missed him entirely, and he laughed, "What's the matter, Female? Haven't figured out how to use your new toy?"

Mandy smiled and strutted confidently toward him. "Yep, I think I've got it totally figured out." Something in her tone caused Green Hand to turn and look … at his shrinking force field, finding it … empty of his intended victims!

Mandy waved her scepter, and team members appeared behind her, shielded from the battle by a powerful yellow force field. She had gathered Gina and Uncle Tyler from their Hummingbirds in one swift motion and placed them behind the force field, along with J.T. and the lizards.

"This battle is between us, Green Hand," Mandy said, waving her scepter again. The astonished wizard found himself transported to a spot before her. "If you want the Lizardstones, take them. From me!"

Mandy stuck her left arm out at him, as if daring him to grab the scepter from her. He paused, obviously trying to decide what she was up to. A moment later, with a sneer spread across his face, he grabbed the scepter with his right hand and worked to wrest it from her grip. The scepter glowed, and the evil wizard watched as some unseen force drew his left hand to grab the scepter. She saw his face strain with an effort to resist, but to no avail. Finally, his left hand gripped the scepter. Mandy smiled and said, with a calm but nasty tone, "What's the matter, Male? Having a problem with my … new toy?" And she grabbed the scepter with her right hand, closed her eyes, and they vanished from the courtyard.

When Mandy next opened her eyes, she and Green Hand were hovering above the fiery inferno of the Abyss. She was calm and in control. He was wide-eyed and panicking in terror. He screamed, "Where are we? What did you do?"

"I brought you to Judgement Day!" declared Mandy. "The scepter can only belong to one of us. Only to those who deserve it. The scepter will decide who is worthy!" With that, Mandy let go of the scepter, watched Green Hand laugh and grab it out of thin air.

"I will destroy you!" Kijani M'kono of Africa shouted in presumed triumph. But then his face turned from a smile of victory to a grimace of pain. "What is happening to me?" he screamed.

An explosion sounded below them, and Mandy watched as a massive hand of flame erupted from the Abyss and grasped Green Hand. Because the scepter judged this wizard to be consumed by evil, it commanded the Abyss to pull him into the flames.

The force from the massive hand of flame threw Mandy from the sky, and she landed on a vast lava escarpment that formed part of the volcano's rim. The scepter lay nearby. Mandy reached out and it flew to her hand. The next instant, the bracelet and the headdress Green Hand had worn appeared on the ground beside her. The Lizardstones burst from the beaded jewelry and circled the scepter! Then Mandy's Dragonstone was pulled from the scepter and replaced by one of the Lizardstones. Finally, Mandy's Dragonstone returned to its place on her cuff bracelet, and the other Lizardstone found its new home on the ring on her left hand.

With four Lizardstones and Gigi's tiger's eye stone embedded in the scepter, Mandy felt a powerful surge of energy fill her body and soul. Looking skyward, she shouted, "I AM OZ, THE GREAT AND POWERFUL!"

Mandy heard her voice echo across the volcano—and then heard voices behind her! She turned, ready for battle, and saw instead that energy beams were firing into the sky from all over her body. Then she heard Phef's voice, "Mandy, you must stop!"

Looking around, she located Phef behind her and slightly to her right. He stood next to Loganna, both with worried looks on their faces. But Mandy felt more powerful, more complete, and more energized than she had ever been in her life. "Fear not. Nothing can stop me! I have more power than anyone else. I can rule the world."

Phef and Loganna exchanged a glance, and then Phef said, "Yes, you could. But, look at where you are." And without warning, Mandy was jerked off the ground and held in place in mid-air, hovering above the Abyss—as the flames from its inferno shot up and around her! With a voice that clearly would brook no argument, Loganna spoke. "Hear me, Mandy. You must resist the power you feel, or the Abyss will consume you completely, as it did to the wizard."

Now, frightened as she watched the flames below her creep closer, Mandy said, "I...I...can't!" It's too strong. It's consuming my every thought! How can I stop this?"

"If anyone can do it, you can, Mandy," a familiar voice said.

Mandy looked back towards Phef and Loganna. Behind them, she saw Gigi and the other ancestors from the Spirit World of Owya. They smiled at her and nodded in agreement as Gigi repeated, "If anyone can do it, you can, Mandy. You are such a wonderful girl, and you are so loved. Think and believe, Mandy! Only love and family can you count on to give you the strength to control that power. All you have to do is think of that as you use your power."

Mandy closed her eyes, focusing on the faces of her loved ones. She felt a shift within herself. The raw, intoxicating surge of magical energy settled, no longer threatening to overwhelm her. Instead, it flowed through her like a gentle river, mighty yet controlled. She opened her eyes, meeting Gigi's gaze. "I understand now," Mandy whispered. "All this power! It's not about ruling or being unstoppable. It's about protecting what matters most."

Gigi nodded, a proud smile on her face. "And what matters most, my dear?"

"Family," Mandy replied without hesitation. "Love. The connections we build." She looked down at the scepter in her hand, its stones glowing softly. "These Lizardstones are not just magical artifacts. They're a legacy - our family's legacy. And with great legacy comes great responsibility."

She took a deep breath, feeling the power settle further, becoming an extension of herself rather than a force trying to control her. "I almost lost myself to it, just like Green Hand did. But our family's love - it anchored me. It reminded me of who I am."

Gigi smiled and reached out to her. "And who are you, Mandy?"

Mandy stood a little straighter, her voice firm with newfound conviction. "I'm Mandy Mandez. Daughter, sister, friend. Protector. And yes, a witch—but one who understands that true power comes from the heart, not just magical ability."

As Mandy embraced this new understanding, she felt the power within her stabilize. The flames of the Abyss receded, and she stood once more on solid ground. Loganna stepped forward, her eyes shining with pride and a hint of tears in them. "You've done what I couldn't, Mandy. You've mastered the power that once consumed me."

Phef nodded solemnly. "And in doing so, you've proven yourself worthy of wielding it. But remember, great power—"

"—comes with great responsibility," Mandy finished, smiling. "I know. And I'm ready."

Gigi hugged Mandy tightly. "It's time for you to go back now, dear. Your family needs you."

Mandy looked around at her spiritual ancestors, feeling a newfound connection to her magical heritage. "Will I see you again?"

Phef assured her. "We're always with you. And now that your connection to this realm has grown stronger, you may find it easier to reach out to us in times of need."

With a last nod of understanding and gratitude, Mandy closed her eyes. She focused on her family, on the Complex, on home. In a flash of yellow light, she vanished from Owya, ready to face whatever challenges lay ahead.

EPILOGUE

D AYS LATER, MEMBERS OF the FDM and the M-Force were cleaning up the mess of the embattled Complex. J.T. had magically repaired the buildings, and Gina and Dr. Kate had assisted the injured. Mickey and Uncle Tyler were repairing the damaged Hummingbirds while Agent Sparks's team tested the security systems and cameras.

A somber mood hung over the group as they worked. Mandy's absence weighed heavily on everyone's minds, though no one dared voice their fears aloud. Mandy's mom suddenly stopped picking up debris, crumpled to a sitting position on the ground, and began crying. Mandy's dad ran to her, knelt beside her, and wrapped his arms around her. The others stopped their work and also gathered around, trying to offer some kind of support.

Suddenly, a familiar voice rang out across the courtyard. "Hi, everyone! I'm back." All activity ceased as heads whipped around to see Mandy standing there, looking exactly as she had before her transformation—no green skin, no towering stature. Just ... Mandy.

Gina was the first to react, rushing forward to embrace her cousin. "Mandy! You're okay!" She pulled back, studying Mandy's face. "But... you're you again. How?"

Mandy's mom slowly approached her daughter, silently embracing her so tightly that Mandy gasped, "Mom, I can't breathe!"

Questions flew as the initial shock, and joy, of Mandy's return settled. Where had she been? What happened to Green Hand? How did she change back?

Mandy held up her hands, a smile spreading across her face. "It's a long story," she said. "Maybe we should sit down." They gathered in a circle, and Mandy began recounting her battle with Green Hand, her trip to Owya, and her encounter with their ancestors. She watched as understanding and awe dawned on their faces.

"So, Loganna... she's not evil anymore?" Uncle Tyler asked, his brow furrowed. Mandy shook her head. "No. She's found peace. And..." she paused, looking at her father, "she's our ancestor. Dad's, mine, Evie's—we are her descendants, and Phef's."

Her father's eyes widened. "Does that mean I could be a wizard, too?" Mandy smiled. "Potentially. But you'd need a Lizardstone, and they're all bonded to me right now."

"Speaking of which," Mickey interjected, "where's the scepter?" Mandy assured them. "It's safe. I can summon it if needed, but I think it's best if it stays hidden for now."

Agent Sparks leaned forward; her expression serious. "Mandy, what you've accomplished is incredible. But it also means our work has only just begun. The magical world is now aware of you. There will be others who might seek to challenge you or exploit your power."

Mandy nodded; her expression was resolute. "I know. But I'm ready. And I have all of you to help me."

"So, what happens now?" little Evie asked, her eyes wide with excitement.

Mandy looked around at her family and friends, feeling a surge of love and gratitude. "Now," she said, "we continue to learn, grow, and protect those who need us. Together."

Unsatisfied, Evie could barely contain her excitement. "Show us ... come on, show us how you can change!"

Mandy looked at the people gathered around her. Family and friends. M-Force and FDM. Comrades in the battle against wrong and evil. They looked at her with smiles and nods, just as her spiritual family had on the volcano rim above the Abyss.

"Alright!" Mandy said. She stood up, raised her left arm into the air, and shouted, "I AM OZ!"

~ The End~

WE'D LOVE TO HEAR FROM YOU

I WOULD LOVE TO GET your feedback on the story you've just read. Hearing from readers of my books is one of the more gratifying things I, as an author, can receive. Contact me at my website (*www.dragonstonestories.com*) or reach out to me on social media (Even Books on Facebook or Mark Even on LinkedIn) and let me know what you think of *The New Lizard Queen*. Or even post a review on Amazon or Goodreads and let everyone know what you think. Reader feedback is important to me as I continue to develop my characters and plotlines. Thank you for your help and thank you for reading this book. I sincerely hope you enjoyed it.

ABOUT
THE AUTHOR

Mark Even is the author of the 4-part Dragonstone Story series of books, ending with *The Destiny of the Lizardstone Scepter*. After his retirement from IBM in 2017, Mark has tapped his interest in stories of fantasy and science fiction and developed the characters and plot lines of the Dragonstone Stories for others to enjoy. Mark and his wife Joyce have also founded a charitable corporation (Healing Chapters Foundation) to provide books to children dealing with illness. When not working on his books or the Foundation, Mark enjoys travel, golf, and being with his family. He is working on a 5th book that will bring new magical adventures to the characters he has created.

www.ingramcontent.com/pod-product-compliance
Lightning Source LLC
Chambersburg PA
CBHW070755120626
46557CB00002B/603